# All Access

## A **Starlet** Novel

# All Access

## A **Starlet** Novel

by Randi Reisfeld

Hyperion Paperbacks
New York

Text copyright © 2007 by Randi Reisfeld

All rights reserved. Published by Hyperion Paperbacks for Children, an imprint of Disney Book Group. No part of this book may be reproduced or transmitted in any form or by any means, electronic or mechanical, including photocopying, recording, or by any information storage and retrieval system, without written permission from the publisher. For information address Hyperion Paperbacks for Children, 114 Fifth Avenue, New York, New York 10011-5690.

First Edition

1 3 5 7 9 10 8 6 4 2

Printed in the United States of America

This book is set in ITC Century Light.

Library of Congress Cataloging-in-Publication Data on file

ISBN-13: 978-14231-0503-9

ISBN-10: 1-4231-0503-6

Visit www.hyperionteens.com

# All Access

**A Starlet Novel**

# Chapter One

## So Pixie Dust!

"Twinkle, twinkle, little Starlet . . ." Matt Canseco said teasingly to Jacey Chandliss. "How I wonder if it's . . . *kismet*?" A swatch of his thick dark hair brushed Jacey's forehead as he leaned over to kiss the tip of her nose.

"Kismet?" Jacey looked into Matt's deep brown eyes. "You mean, fate? Like, you and me being together is kismet? Or . . ."—she reached up to trace his curvy lips with her fingertip—"is 'kismet' the only word you can think of that *almost* rhymes with 'starlet'?"

"Busted," Matt admitted with a grin. "What I meant was, you look especially luminescent tonight."

"I wonder," Jacey mused, "if *that's* because I'm gazing at a perfect Malibu sunset from a secluded beach cove—

and because I'm making out with the world's hottest movie star."

"That's all I am to you, Dimples?" Matt harrumphed, pretending to be insulted. "Just some hot movie star?"

"No way!" Jacey scoffed. "You're my *personal* hot movie star. Besides, did you not just call me a starlet? As in: just another of the dozens of sweet young actresses that Matt Canseco has conquered?"

*The last one* was what Jacey hoped he'd say; that he'd saved the best for last. 'Cause she'd done what no one before her could have: persuaded the relationship-phobic actor to *admit* that he was way into her and then *commit* to not dating anyone else. He was in love, for the first time. With her.

But Matt didn't say all that. He planted his elbow in the sand, leaned over, and got up in her face. In a good way.

Their kiss was heavenly, like the sparkling sand beneath them, the gentle ocean in front of them, and the sky: a mesmerizing mural of pinks and corals that was quickly giving way to blazing orange. The sunset had come to symbolize Los Angeles for Jacey—that and the trees in people's backyards, which were heavy with oranges, lemons, and limes. Even out here, at the water's edge, the air was tinged with the scent of citrus.

Jacey nestled into the soft part of Matt's bronzed

chest, her cheek resting beneath his shoulder. His arm slipped around her; she could feel each beat of his heart. Her own swelled with happiness. And so much gratitude.

She felt as if she'd been sprinkled with pixie dust.

Jacey Chandliss, seventeen years old, had arrived in Los Angeles the previous April, having come from Bloomfield Hills, Michigan. She'd won the prize on a brand-new TV reality show called *Generation Next: The Search for America's Top Young Actor*, where, as on *American Idol*, the viewers voted to select the winner. Her prize had been a role in a major motion picture, and, after filming, she'd come back to L.A. for the glitzy Hollywood premiere. She'd decided to stay through the summer, partly to audition for other movies, but mainly to kick it Cali-style with her best friends, who'd come with, since her parents could not. There was money, freedom, and fun in the sun. Jacey and her crew had figured on a three-month fantasy vacation. It was now late November.

So much had happened!

The movie she'd won the part in, *Four Sisters*, had opened to glowing reviews. Jacey, once a TV-viewers' favorite, had become Hollywood's new It girl. She'd been deluged with movie scripts; each studio offered to pay more than the last. And she had been nominated for a Teen Choice Award! She hadn't won, but the experience had been awesomely unforgettable. She'd acted onstage in an edgy play and gotten great reviews. She had finished her second movie, a space action film called *Galaxy Rangers*. Even though she had regrets about that one, she was already signed to a big-time contract for several more films.

Her acting future was set. Right now, life was idyllic.

There was Malibu. From the moment she'd set foot in the sand, Jacey had felt as if she'd come home—albeit to a place she'd never been, except in her head.

And there was Matt.

She'd been into *him* from the minute they'd first met. His dreamy, brooding good looks and sinewy, compact bod probably had something to do with it.

The best thing about Matt was that he "got" her—all of her: Jacey the actress and Jacey the girl. He was the one straight guy she could talk to about anything. That is, when she wasn't otherwise occupied, as was the case now. She was responding hungrily to a fresh wave of Matt's passionate kisses and soft caresses.

Jacey wanted to give Matt more than kisses. God knows. Just not . . . yet.

She didn't have to explain it.

"It's okay." Matt tried to steady his breathing. "Not trying to push you. It's just that I haven't seen you all weekend. Feels like forever."

"For me, too, Matt," Jacey murmured, nuzzling up against him. "It's just that it's so new. *We're* so new."

Jacey's insta-attraction had not led to insta-coupledom. Everyone had said Matt was bad for her; Matt himself had warned Jacey that he'd end up breaking her heart. He had, too. But then he'd mended it, and they'd both caved in to the truth: they were meant for each other.

Jacey had just come back from Michigan, where she'd spent Thanksgiving weekend with her family—her mom, quite pregnant, couldn't travel—while Matt remained in Los Angeles.

"How'd it go, anyway?" he asked now. "Do your parents know you've acquired your own personal movie star?"

"The *National Enquirer* and the *Star* revealed that info for me," she said wryly. "The only thing they didn't report is that I spent every minute thinking of you, wishing you'd been there."

"That probably wouldn't have been a good idea. Don't think I'm what your family has in mind for you, little Miss Wholesome."

"My family rocks!" Jacey exclaimed. "They see people, not stereotypes. If they thought you were going to hurt me, or get me into trouble, they'd be all over you like bubble gum on sneaker soles."

Matt smiled ruefully. "You do realize how lucky you are, Dimples? Most stage parents care only about three things: the money, the money, and—the money! You have no idea how many of them push their kids into showbiz, see all that green, then steal from them."

"I refuse to believe that—" Jacey began. Then she rethought. "Is that what happened to you?"

Matt seemed taken aback by the directness of her question. "No, not exactly. But that's what went down for a lot of kids I know."

Matt had started appearing in movies at the age of thirteen—eight years earlier. He never talked about his childhood, and in the few times they'd been alone together, the subject hadn't come up. It was only by accident that Jacey had learned that Matt supported his grandfather. As far as she knew, Matt had spent his Thanksgiving with friends.

Jacey continued to probe. "Did your parents . . ." She paused, not sure how to continue. ". . . Did they support your acting dreams?"

Matt laughed and shook his head. "Oh, Dimples,

sometimes I forget how sheltered you are. It wasn't like that. I grew up with my dad, and I was pretty much on my own."

"Where's your mom?"

"Six feet under," he said. "Same as your biological dad, I guess."

Now it was Jacey's turn to be taken aback. "Why do you assume he's dead?"

"You always talk about your stepdad," Matt said with a shrug. "I figured your real dad would be in the picture somewhere if your parents were divorced. Now that you're a famous . . ."—he paused to tweak her nose—". . . starlet."

Jacey scowled. "You should leave the detective work to the professionals." She was suddenly annoyed—why?

"Whoa, didn't mean to touch a nerve."

Jacey pondered what Matt had just said. The truth was, she had no idea where her biological father, Jake Chandliss, was or even *if* he was.

"You've never been curious?" Matt—who clearly *was*—pressed. "Never tried to find him? I'd think the actor in you would be very interested."

"He's just not part of my life. It doesn't come up."

"And he's never tried to find you?"

"No! Why would he?" Detective Canseco *was* starting to get on her nerves.

"Winning *Generation* is like hitting the lotto," Matt said. "Everyone thinks you're rich. Relatives come out of the woodwork when they think you have money."

"Not mine," Jacey said. "The only creatures that crawled out of the woodwork were the paparazzi."

"Why are you so sensitive about it, then?" Matt asked.

"I don't know." She couldn't keep the irritation out of her voice. "My mom struggled so hard when I was a kid—which is when he left—and then everything changed when she met Larry. He was so great to us. I love him to pieces, and he treats me like a daughter. Always has."

"He didn't adopt you, though," Matt pointed out. "Or you'd be using his last name."

Jacey crinkled her forehead. "Adopt me? I never thought about it." Then she brightened. "Maybe Larry could adopt me now!" She was only half kidding.

"Aren't you a little old for that?"

"You know exactly how old I am, Matt Canseco."

Only a few weeks earlier, he had been citing the age difference between them—she was seventeen and he, twenty-one—as a reason they shouldn't be together.

"Barely legal—that's how young you are." Matt nibbled her earlobe. "But you'll be eighteen soon. And then . . ." He left off, suggestively.

She knew the rest of the sentence. *Then* she'd have no reason to hold back. Did Matt think she was waiting to turn eighteen to have sex? Maybe, she mused, *he* was the one waiting for her to reach a lawful age.

Like all hot young actors, Matt had an image—made up by the press, fueled by his R-rated indie movies, and believed by the public. But the whole bad-boy thing wasn't completely bogus. Matt *did* have a tendency to trash hotel rooms, think with his fists, drink too much on occasion, and—prior to meeing her, of course—date scary-looking Goth girls and/or scary-looking models.

Matt claimed that the real reason for his brooding image was his refusal to play the Hollywood game. A for-real independent spirit, Matt didn't do red carpets, swag bags, or designer duds. "Watching all those rich, beautiful people congratulating themselves makes me sick," he had told Jacey. "Besides, actors shouldn't be competing against one another. It's stupid."

Matt also nixed starring in big-budget popcorn movies. He had the acting chops to rival anyone in his age group, combined with looks to equal those of heart-breakers like Leo, Brad, and Johnny. Naturally, Hollywood had wanted to put him up on billboards, plaster him all over the teen magazines, and completely objectify him (as he put it), but he'd refused. He'd said no to the money, the fame, the spotlight. His latest movie was a gritty psychological thriller called *Dirt Nap*.

Matt Canseco wouldn't be talking to *Access Hollywood* about it; he wouldn't even talk to *Rolling Stone*. He didn't have a Web site or a MySpace page. He said that all publicity was evil and detracted from the art.

Jacey had an image, too. Hers was that of a wholesome, all-American nice girl. It had been foisted upon her by the people who'd made her famous in the first place—the *Generation Next* team. Jacey's agent worked to make sure she played to that image, deciding which movies she'd do, what she'd say in interviews, and how she'd look when photographed.

In the end, and most irretrievably, Jacey's image had been formed by her fans. She was the people's choice—they'd voted for her and taken her into their hearts as America's sweetheart. She owed her fantastic new life to them and had little choice but to heed her advisers and maintain her image.

The dark truth was that she didn't always mind. A lot of it was fun.

At the end of the day, Jacey and Matt weren't their images—they weren't all that far from those images, either. That made for some fundamental differences between the two of them. But Jacey believed that love and passion easily conquered those. This might not have been a bad time to test that theory, she thought, repositioning herself behind Matt to massage his shoulders.

"Mmmm . . . that feels good," Matt murmured. "If your acting career nose-dives, you could make it as a massage therapist."

"Nose-dives, huh? That could happen sooner than we think. The *Galaxy Rangers* premiere is coming up soon. I'm so nervous about it!"

Matt reached up to his shoulders, covering her hands with his. "Maybe *Galaxy* won't be that bad."

"Yeah, maybe I'll win an Academy Award for it. C'mon, Matt, we all know that movie was a bad choice. A fact that will be painfully obvious when it goes straight to video."

"Don't sweat it, we all make bad choices sometimes—" he started to console her, but Jacey cut him off.

"I could really use your support, Matt."

He swung around to face her. "Anything, Dimples."

"Anything as in, you'll come to the premiere with me?" she asked hopefully.

Matt seemed surprised by her request.

Jacey soldiered on. "I know you never do this stuff— red carpet, schmoozing with the press, but I was thinking . . ." She traced a line down his ropy bicep with her finger.

". . . If you said yes, we could do ourselves a favor, too."

"What's that?" Matt asked warily.

"This would be our first public appearance as a couple. We wouldn't be as interesting to the paparazzi if we were open about our relationship, instead of waiting for them to catch us in the act."

"I see you've given this a lot of thought, Dimples," Matt said, running his fingers through his hair.

"So what do you say? For me? For us?" She moved in closer and brushed her lips against his.

"Can I think about it?"

"Of course," Jacey said, wrapping her arms around his neck.

# jaceyfan blog

## Jacey's Secrets-Exposed!

I'm back—your secret source for everything Jacey! I'll tell you all the stuff she doesn't want you to know . . . even though it's your *Gen Next* right! I'm so inside, I scoop the tabloids. . . .

Didja miss me over Thanksgiving? Matt C. sure missed Jacey, and gave thanks indeed when she returned—via a prolonged make-out session in the cove they still think is private. . . . C'mon, guys. Give me a challenge!

Speaking of Thanksgiving, I'm hearing that the real turkey will be released next month. I speak, of course, of *Galaxy Rangers*, about to soar into a theater near you, then hit the ground hard, in smokin' shards. For those of you with short memories, or who need a Jacey tutorial, this is only her second movie. Will she go from darling newcomer to money-grubbing has-been, all in under a year? Gobble, gobble!

# Chapter Two

## To Posse [verb]: To Protect and Defend— and Agree with—Starlet, Whether She Is Right or Wrong

The next morning, Jacey awoke to the scrumptious aroma of freshly baked cinnamon buns wafting up through the window of her second-floor bedroom. She would have bet there were bagels, muffins, and chocolate croissants, too—delivered straight from the oven by her new favorite bakery, Malibuns.

When she'd lived in Bloomfield Hills, she had called her closest friends her BFFs. In Hollywood, they were known as her posse. No matter what she called them, they were the people she trusted most. Her peeps loved to eat, and since they'd all taken up residence in pricey Malibu, fast food and leftovers were just a memory. Now, they ate only mouthwatering munchies of the expensive kind. It was all about fitting in, they told her. Anyone in Malibu who didn't employ a private chef had to have all their meals freshly prepared and delivered. That was how Malibuans rolled.

Jacey stretched and hopped out of bed. Her room had a choice, ocean-facing balcony. Leaning over the curved railing gave her a full view of the deck, where her posse was doing breakfast.

A lean girl with never-ending legs and vampy green eyes was nibbling the top of a cinnamon bun, using her laptop as a tray for her grande latte. This was posse member number one: Jacey's cousin, Ivy Langhorne. Nearly twenty-two years old, Ivy had graduated from college the previous year with one degree and zero job prospects. She'd jumped at the chance to accompany Jacey to Los Angeles, where she would act as legal guardian, chaperone, and family-anointed protectress.

That had been the idea, anyway.

Somewhere along the way, Ivy had fallen head over heels in love—with the Hollywood scene *and* with a 23-year-old L.A. native named Emilio Perez. Ivy liked to shop, and she liked to be waited on and pampered. She quickly became the posse's entitlement queen. In the process, she chose a career path, too. She wanted to work for a big agency, handling stars' careers. She'd just started an internship with Jacey's agent, Cinnamon T. Jones.

In direct contrast to the toned, focused Ivy was posse pal number two: Desiree Paczi, Jacey's best friend for mostly ever. Desi, using her belly as a plate, was stretched out on a lounge chair, contentedly munching away on a flaky croissant. The ringleted eighteen-year-old was loyal, funny, petite, and round. She did her best to keep it real. Like, really real. As in, square-peg-in-a-round-hole real—or, bull-in-a-china-shop real. Desi was never gonna fit in out here. Nor was she interested in trying. She remained a healthy contrast to Hollywood's obsession with skinny. Unlike Ivy's instant "gimme more" embrace of life in the excess lane, Desi still reacted to things as the working-class girl she was.

There was the outburst in the fancy Beverly Hills restaurant: "Twenty-three dollars for vegetable soup? What's in it, real gold?" Well-coiffed heads had turned!

There was the too-fast Mercedes that Desi had wrecked by banging it into a Beverly Hills park statue.

There was the exchanging of her first-class ticket to Las Vegas for two seats in coach—so she could bring along her surfer-dude summer fling, Mike.

There were also the two bar brawls (that they knew about).

Desi hadn't learned the art of the withering stare and the cutting remark. When confronting a perceived rival, girlfriend reacted with her fists.

Desi always meant well; she would have done anything for Jacey—that included the crucial task of keeping the starlet from going totally Hollywood—a job for which Ivy was no longer fit.

Rounding out the posse-pack was the cappuccino-sipping Dashiell Walker. Dash and Jacey, next-door neighbors since kindergarten, had a fraternal bond. They were each other's best confidantes. Curly-haired, hazel-eyed Dash, like Ivy, was finding life, liberty, and the pursuit of happiness more fulfilling out here than back at home. Dash had found his first serious boyfriend here in Cali.

"Hey, down there, wanna leave some crumbs for me?" Jacey called out.

Three heads snapped upward at the same time. All wore dark shades—so L.A.! Of course, it was a sparkling, cloudless Malibu morning, with just a hint of a chill in the air.

Jacey instantly detected another chill—as in, vibe—rising off her friends. No one smiled or offered a jokey comeback. It was too quiet down there. Where was the music, which usually went into surround sound as soon as Desi woke up? Possibly, something wasn't altogether marvelous on this majestic Malibu morn. Maybe they weren't feasting so much as carb-loading: 'cause Ivy, Desi, and Dash looked pissed off and ready to rumble.

"When I get my hands on that blogger, I will take him down!" Desi growled, her eyes fixed on her Helio screen. "It's one thing to spread lies about your personal life, Jace—but when he starts attacking your acting, that's going too far!" The flakes of croissant crumbs dusting her chest did undermine Desi's threatening tone a bit.

Instead of rushing downstairs to deal with her friends' anger, Jacey took a shower, washed her hair, and turned the music on. Feeling refreshed, she put on her retro pink and black Elvis drawstring pajama bottoms and a tank top, then went down to make her deckside appearance.

Desi was still railing at the day's serving of blogger bull. Dash was nervously pecking away on his BlackBerry. Ivy looked even grumpier up close than she had from a distance. Jacey refused to get sucked into their bad moods. She'd had one of the best nights of her life the night before with Matt—even if he hadn't exactly committed to being her arm candy at the premiere. And now, there was that yummy, already-prepared breakfast. The beach was at her doorstep, the ocean just a few yards away. Again, pixie dust!

Yes, the anonymous blogger had been the bane of her nearly perfect existence ever since she had arrived in Hollywood. So he had attacked her acting again? Was that the best he could come up with? Pff!

Snapping her fingers in time to the music, she danced around the deck.

"Come on, you guys," she urged them, "don't be so bummed."

Desi looked up at her, astounded. "Have you even seen what he wrote?"

"Don't know. Don't care." Jacey's posse had become blogger addicts. Wasn't admitting it the first step? The first thing they did each morning was check out what new outrageous lie had been written about Jacey. Was there a rehab for that kind of addiction? 'Cause they'd all stopped paying attention to the tabloids and the paparazzi. Their obsession was blogger-specific. It was probably extra-interesting to them because, whoever he was, he claimed to have inside info about Jacey and, too often now, actually did. Exposing this anonymous creep had leaped to the top of their to-do lists.

The bogus blogger alone wasn't usually enough to freak her friends out. Especially not Desi.

This morning, there was also a video.

"You're all the rage on YouTube," Ivy said flatly. "And

not in a good way. So maybe you will care."

YouTube, the Web destination for homemade videos? Jacey stopped in the middle of her dance. The paparazzi hadn't secretly videotaped her and Matt last night, had they? What if they'd recorded their conversation, too? She sank into a chair and braced herself. "What's on it?"

"Something that might prove the blogger—that he-she-it monster—right," Ivy grumbled.

"What do you mean?" Jacey asked unsteadily. Desi had just accused the blogger of attacking her acting. If the YouTube video was some old audition, or a video of her back in Michigan, it would be embarrassing but not exactly the end of the world.

"What do you mean, 'prove the blogger right'?" Desi snarled at Ivy. "You think this YouTube video proves she's a bad actress?"

"Whoa. Down, girl," Dash said. "It's just not the most flattering clip."

"Clip?" That didn't sound like her and Matt. Whew! "Whatever it is, gimme here." Jacey held her arms out toward Ivy.

Ivy sighed and handed the laptop over.

Instantly, Jacey saw what was freaking everyone out. It was under YouTube's Featured Videos. The title was "Sneak a Peek at *Galaxy Rangers!*"

"Unless it's the trailer, this shouldn't be on here," Jacey mumbled.

"Trust me, cousin, the trailer it's not," said Ivy.

As soon as the music began, Jacey knew exactly what the sneak peek was. She braced herself. The screen became filled with a close-up of her as Zorina, the futuristic space-patroller–slash–hero. That was embarrassing enough. Also on screen was Zartagnian, her male partner. The scene had been added at the last minute, and she'd fought against its inclusion. It was the love scene. The stupid, nonsensical love scene.

Watching it now, her stomach sank. This was a train wreck. Both she and Adam Pratt, the actor who played Zartagnian, looked like third-grade doofuses. She'd barely had been able to contain her laughter when they'd filmed the take, and it showed on screen. Ugh! And that awful shade of lip gloss they'd made her wear. Jacey hadn't thought it could look any worse than she remembered, but in a close-up? If heinous were a color, this would be it.

Jacey turned away before the actual lip lock.

"Is it possible this is bogus?" Dash offered hopefully. "Some parody perpetuated by a jokester?"

Jacey shook her head. "If only. Now you understand why I fought so hard against doing this scene."

Ivy tried to take the laptop away before Jacey was able

to check out the sure-to-be-cruel viewer comments.

"You can't pull this away from me now." Jacey knew she was being masochistic, but she couldn't help herself.

Under "Rate This Video," the stolen *Galaxy Rangers* clip had gotten half a star out of four. Viewer comments ranged from "What a hoot! Who said Jacey couldn't do comedy?" to "The actors' lack of chemistry is obvious. If this scene is representative of the rest of the movie, I say, 'skip it!'" There was also this recycled gem: "To say their acting is wooden is an insult to puppets everywhere."

"Can't we just lie and say it's a fake?" Desi looked serious. "Celebrities always deny things until there's proof."

"Can we counter with something?" Dash asked Ivy.

Jacey returned the laptop to Ivy. "You know what, guys? Let's just forget it. The studio will take it down any minute. And sue whoever's responsible for the leak."

"It's too late!" Ivy threw her hands up in frustration. "Half the world's already seen it. They think the movie's a joke."

Jacey refused to be freaked out. The truth was, she didn't care all that much about how she looked in the clip and cared even less about how Adam looked. She just felt sorry for the movie's director, Emory Farber. It was his reputation that would suffer the most. She glanced at Ivy. "Call Cinnamon, and be sure they're blacking this out."

Ivy shut the computer. "Done."

"Very funny. Now, can I eat? Did you guys leave me anything?"

Desi handed her the end of a croissant. "Sorry. That's all that's left. I stress-eat."

Dash passed her a muffin.

Jacey ate them both, then washed them down with a glass of freshly squeezed grapefruit juice.

"How can you be so casual?" Ivy asked. "Don't you care if you become a laughingstock?"

"Overreacting much?" Jacey asked. "It's just one stupid scene from one stupid movie. It's not my whole career, and it's certainly not my life."

Ivy's jaw dropped. "Not your life? I thought acting *was* your life, Jacey."

"She's in love: L-U-V," Desi sang, quoting an old pop song. "Nothing can bring her down, not while M-A-T-T is around."

"What's love got to do with it?" Ivy returned drily. "Seriously, Jace, we have to talk, Cinnamon's been calling nonstop."

"Why does *that* not surprise me?" Jacey rolled her eyes. To her agent, there was no middle ground. Everything was epic: either FABULOUS! or A DISASTER! The YouTube clip qualified as the latter.

"Listen, cousin," Ivy said. "*You* may not be unglued by the YouTube thing, but your bosses are. They want spin control, and they want it now."

"Let's try that in English," Jacey deadpanned.

"They want to announce that you've chosen your next movie. That'll turn into the big news, making everyone forget about this thing," Dash translated.

No, Jacey thought, the real this-just-in bulletin would be her and Matt, arm in arm on the red carpet at the premiere. Maybe they'd even kiss for the cameras. That would make everyone forget the *Galaxy* clip! She licked her lips dreamily.

"Earth to Jacey, get your head out of the clouds," Ivy said. "You have a press conference tomorrow."

"No way," Jacey said. "Tomorrow is promised to *Generation Next*. Or did you guys forget that I accepted their invitation to be a guest judge for this year's competition?"

"No one's forgotten anything," Ivy said. "You're multitasking."

"Fine. What am I announcing?"

"That's what we're trying to tell you," Desi said, in an attempt to fill her in. "You're gonna announce your next big movie."

"But I haven't even chosen it yet. . . . Have I?" She

eyed her friends suspiciously. Ever since Ivy had begun her internship and Dash had started acting as her unofficial manager—and, okay, ever since she'd started obsessing about Matt—Jacey accepted that certain decisions were being made for her. The fact that she trusted Ivy, Dash, and Desi made that all right.

"What are my choices?" Jacey asked.

Ivy unzipped her humongous Vuitton pouch, pulled out a stack of scripts, and handed them to Jacey.

Using her knees as a book rest, Jacey browsed through them. They were all action-fantasy films. The deal she'd made with Avalon Studios required her to star in superhero movies. She got to choose which one. In exchange, she would get three things: gobs of money; the right to make smaller, independent films, like Matt did; *und* a big donation made by the studio on her behalf to the charity of her choice.

She hadn't made that choice yet. Dash was supposed to help her.

Now, she rattled off the titles of the scripts in front of her: "*Wonder Woman*; *Alien Meets Elektra*; *The Return of Supergirl*; *Princess Zorro*." Not one of them appealed to her. Jacey looked up at her three best friends. They'd so already made the decision for her.

"And the winner is . . . ?"

## This Just In!

It's a bird, it's a plane, it's Jacey in spin control! Check it out, Jaceyfans, here comes headline news. Minutes ago, Jacey wrapped a lively press conference announcing that she'll star in *The Return of Supergirl*.

Jacey Chandliss, action hero! Wholesome good-girl, fighting for truth, justice, and the American way! Whoo-*hoo*! Finally, something we, the fans, want to see. Not the cartoon buffoon from *Galaxy Rangers*, not the homeless punk she turned herself into for that nasty play last summer. Supergirl! Either she's finally listening to her fans, or her handlers have knocked some sense into her stubborn little head.

I'll give her this: Jacey gets courage-cred for putting it out there live and uncensored, when she could have made a Web site announcement. She had to know that all the questions from reporters were gonna be about YouTube and Matt Canseco.

Here's an eyewitness account (Yup, I was there,

right under her nose!): after being introduced as the newest starlet at Avalon Studios, Jacey ascended to the podium. She wore crimson knee-high boots, patterned tights under a miniskirt, a fitted blue T-shirt, and her dimply smile. Acting like she didn't have a care in the world, she waved to fans and posed for the cameras, tossing her long, copper tresses. Team Jacey—agent Cinnamon Jones, publicist Peyton Spinner, acolytes Ivy Langhorne, Dash Walker, and Desi Paczi—quickly surrounded her.

Turns out, she didn't need all that support. Her performance was Golden Globe–worthy. Too bad she'll never get one for *Galaxy Rangers*! But I digress. Jacey did her thing, charming and disarming all of the press conference invitees.

"How cool is this?" Jacey gushed when the applause died down. "I get to slip into the high-heeled boots of one of the strongest, most powerful girl characters ever written. Even better is that the new movie lets me play two roles, Kara Zor-El (that's Supergirl's Kryptonian name) *and* Linda Danvers, her secret identity. It's scary and exciting to portray characters people already know and love. I just hope I'm worthy. I want to create a hero that young girls can look up to."

Here's a reality check, Jaceyfans. It's all an act. I happen to know that she's not at all thrilled about *Supergirl*. She'd much rather be in some pervy indie, or anything else that would keep her close to Matt Canseco.

Okay, back to fantasyland. Out strutted the big photo op: movie hunk Brandon Routh, the brawny, blue-eyed star of the current Superman movies, to join Jacey at the podium. Cheese alert: he tied a red cape around her shoulders and "welcomed" her to the Super-family. Then Jacey twirled in the cape, displaying the big *S* on the back. Can I barf now?

Now for the juicy part: question-and-answer time. Reporters fired away, and Jacey didn't duck them. Not that she really answered honestly. She only made it look that way.

Q: Did you see YouTube yesterday?

A: Unfortunately.

Q: What did you think of the *Galaxy Rangers* clip?

A: I threw the laptop over the balcony! Just kidding. But I was upset. I wish it hadn't been leaked. I hope it's been taken down.

Q: Are you embarrassed about how you looked in that scene?

A: On my personal list of most embarrassing moments, it was barely a glitch. Since I got to Hollywood, my life feels like bumper-to-bumper bloopers.

Q: Is *Galaxy* as bad as it looks?

A: I hope no one judges an entire movie by one stolen snippet of a scene. A scene that might not even make the final cut. But am I ashamed, or embarrassed? Not a chance, Lance. I'm proud of all the work everyone did on this movie, and especially of Emory Farber, our director. We tried to make an entertaining movie. When it comes out, the audience will let us know if we succeeded.

O-kay! Jacey succeeded in shutting down that line of questioning! But the reporters weren't done with her.

Q: What's going on between you and Matt Canseco?

A: We're friends. So far, we haven't come to blows.

Q: You made a couple of lists this month. Worst

dressed. Most overexposed. And your drunk dancing in the Las Vegas video tied with Britney's baldie, Paris's DUI, and Lindsay's post-appendix party for Who's Trying Hardest to Kill Her Career? How do you react to those?

A: With great glee! In this town, those are compliments. I really *am* a starlet!

# Chapter Three

## Desi's Got a Secret. Make That Two.

"What's an a-CO-lit?" asked Desi, scrunching her forehead in confusion as she read the blogger's eyewitness account of Jacey's *Supergirl* announcement off her Helio. Desi and Jacey had hopped into a waiting limo right after the press conference and were headed for Jacey's next appointment, at the *Generation Next* set.

"*AC*-o-lite," said Jacey. "It means 'assistant.'" She leaned back against the plush leather seat of the stretch Cadillac and sipped her raspberry iced tea.

"Oh," Desi said. "I figured it was an insult."

It was, Jacey thought. The blundering blogger probably thought he was saying "lackey."

Desi scanned the rest of the blog. "Okay. It's not

that bad. The worst he writes is that you were faking it."

*So* true.

Jacey had about as much interest in donning Supergirl tights as she had in flipping burgers at Mickey D's. But a deal was a deal, and she'd been brought up to honor hers to the best of her ability.

"Otherwise," added Desi, "you came off pretty good—for a change."

"I'll be sure to send the blogger a thank-you note."

"You got a bunch of messages. Want me to read them?"

"Go for it," Jacey yawned.

*I couldn't have handled it better,* texted Peyton. Coming from a power publicist, that was high praise.

*FABULOUS!* summed up Cinnamon's reaction.

*We're so proud of our newest star,* was the gushy message from the head of Avalon Studios.

Might they send her a gift? Jacey wondered. Big movie studios often did that. Not that she needed or wanted anything.

*You showed 'em, Dimples.* A smile spread across Jacey's face—the first genuine one of the day.

"How sweet is he?" Jacey went all warm and fuzzy inside. "I have to text him back."

"Listen," Desi said hesitantly as Jacey pecked away at the tiny keyboard. "I have a couple . . . a thing . . .

of things . . . some stuff to talk to you about."

Jacey raised an eyebrow. It wasn't like Desi to fumble for words. "Serious stuff?"

"Um, sort of. Some."

Jacey braced herself. Uh-oh. What had Des done now? And how much would it cost to repair the damage?

Desi drew a long breath. "Um, first, I know it's a busy day already, but I kind of made an appointment for us after the *Generation Next* thing."

Please don't let it be at a lawyer's, was Jacey's first thought. "Appointment with who? Is someone suing us, Des?"

Desi looked shocked. "Of course not! Why would you think that? No, we're going to a place called Shelter Rock."

Jacey flipped through her mental Rolodex. "Why does that sound familiar?"

"'Cause we used to look at pictures in *Us Weekly* and *Teen People* back when celebrities held benefits for it. We'd make fun of what everyone was wearing— remember?"

Jacey did. That was when *she* wasn't the one being criticized. "Shelter Rock. It's an orphanage or something?"

"Not exactly," Desi said. "It's a temporary shelter for kids who can't stay with their parents—sometimes their folks are in jail, or they get sick, or they were abusive. Shelter Rock keeps the kids there."

"Sounds worthy," Jacey allowed. "And we're going there today, why?"

"Um, it'd be a good charity for you to promote—to give money to. You still want to do that, right?"

"Of course . . ." Jacey conceded, "but—"

"So I made an appointment for you with Rosalie Cross, the woman who runs Shelter Rock. Just to check it out," Desi explained. "I told them we'd come after the *Generation Next* taping."

Jacey felt uneasy. Something about the way Desi had gone about this—almost covertly—felt weird. As if it were a secret. Jacey had specifically chosen Dash to help figure out which charities to support, because he was always thorough, methodical, and rational.

Desi, on the other hand, was a total soft touch. She did everything impulsively, guided by her heart, not her head. Now she was staring hopefully at Jacey.

"Does Dash know about this?" Jacey tried to sound casual.

Desi fumbled. "Not exactly. Yet."

"Okay, Desiree, what are you not telling me?"

"Nothing!" the cherub-cheeked girl crossed her arms defensively.

Desi was lying. There was more to this. And it would come out soon enough—Desi couldn't keep a secret to save her life. "Okay, Des, it's fine," Jacey said. "This seems to be important to you, so, sure, I'm happy to go see Shelter Rock and meet whoever you want. Okay?"

Relief spread across Desi's face. Impulsively, she leaned over to give Jacey a peck on the cheek.

"So we're good?" Jacey asked, slouching in her seat and closing her eyes.

"There's something else," Desi said slowly. "It's about Emilio."

"As in . . . Ivy's Emilio?"

"Maybe not so much anymore," Desi responded grimly.

Jacey snapped to attention. "What's going on?" Her cousin and Emilio had been together practically from the day they met. In spite of their height difference (it was so cute that he came up to her shoulder), they seemed joined at the hip. Privately, Jacey called them Ivilio.

"It's not good. She's gonna be hurt," Desi answered darkly, "when—or if—she finds out."

"Finds out . . ." Jacey paused. "Wait a minute, no way! He's cheating? How do you know?"

"Dash told me. He got it from Aja, who saw Emilio hooking up with some random dancer. Emilio admitted it

right away when Aja confronted him. He wasn't even trying to hide it."

Jacey sat up straight, letting the information sink in.
Neither Dash nor his boyfriend, Aja, traded in gossip.
If it hadn't been eyewitnessed, they wouldn't have passed
it on.

"What should we do?" asked Desi nervously. "Tell
her?"

Jacey was furious. How come Matt hadn't told *her*?
Emilio was his best friend! She started to speed-dial him,
but stopped herself.

"Don't tell her?" Desi guessed. "Maybe it's a onetime
thing?"

"Someone has to tell her," Jacey said, shaking her
head slowly, "but I'm not so sure it should be us. Emilio
should man up. Either confess and beg her forgiveness, or
tell her he . . ."—she shook her head again, sadly—"wants
to end it."

"So we don't say anything?" Desi was surprised.

"We stay close—to pick up the pieces."

# Chapter Four

## The Next *Generation*

"It's her! It's really *her!*" A fragile-looking girl burst into tears when Jacey walked through the dressing room door backstage at *Generation Next*.

"This is so cool! I can't believe it!" A curvy, bling-bedecked blond exclaimed.

Jacey, still distracted by the Emilio newsflash, was confused for a minute. "What's up with the drama?" she asked Desi. She was supposed to be meeting the four contestants who were battling it out for the title of America's Top Young Actor. Had she wandered into the wrong dressing room by accident?

Desi elbowed her. "You're the drama. You're the first winner—like Kelly Clarkson—the poster child for who they could be. They've been dying to meet you!"

But . . . they were so *young*! They looked like fans. They *acted* like fans. Jacey, having seen just a few clips of the show that season, was vaguely familiar with the finalists, but backstage they seemed so ordinary. One of these four would really follow in her L.A.M.B. sneakers? Tiny Tears? Bling-blond? One of the guys hovering behind them? Seriously? At Desi's nudging, Jacey smiled and took a step toward the foursome, hand extended.

"Hey, it's great to meet you," Jacey said, scouring her memory for their names. Desi had forgotten to coach her in the car. Jacey was fairly sure that the freckled boy with the curly red hair was named Todd.

"Todd Forest," he said, stepping forward to take her outstretched hand. "Where's your entourage?"

Jacey pointed to Desi. "You're looking at her."

"All the big stars come with bodyguards, and everyone knows you have a posse," Crystal Bleu, the screamer with the bracelets, sparkly earrings, and multiple necklaces, said. She seemed disappointed.

"My friend Dash is in school right now," Jacey explained. "At UCLA—he's a freshman—and my cousin Ivy is at work. She's an intern at my agency."

"Really?" Todd, who had huge brown eyes and curly red eyelashes, seemed shocked. "Like regular people?"

"Yep, school and work. Still regular people."

Desi stepped up. "And don't underestimate me just because I'm short. I give good bodyguard."

Everyone laughed. P. J. Chang was the teary one, and Garrett McKinley, the quiet one with scruffy blond hair, completed the foursome. They settled on the dressing-room couch, hands in their laps, stars in their eyes. They looked at Jacey expectantly, as if she could wave a magic wand and poof, make one of them famous.

Is that what *I* looked like? she wondered. Just one year ago she'd sat on that same couch waiting, hoping, praying that she'd win. It seemed like a lifetime had gone by.

"You guys, you remind me of . . . just exactly how it was for me!" Jacey was really moved. When she'd agreed to guest-judge, it hadn't occurred to her that it would pack such an emo-wallop. Was it because the dressing room was exactly the same, down to the ripped pleather couch and mismatched armchairs? Was that why she felt teary, and—to use a Cinnamon word—*verklempt*?

"You weren't as nervous as we are," declared P.J., a sparrow of a girl whose long, straight bangs nearly obscured her eyes.

"I was petrified every single day," Jacey exclaimed. "My stomach was in constant churn cycle, and my heart thumped so loudly I was sure the TV microphones picked it up all the way from the dressing room."

P.J. covered her mouth with a delicate hand and giggled nervously.

"It never showed," asserted Todd.

"She's an actress, people!" Desi piped up; then she added—since, unlike Jacey, *she* hadn't missed a single week of that season's *Generation Next* competition— "None of you seem nervous when you're onstage, either."

That comment sparked a spirited rebuttal from the finalists.

"So, what was your secret—how did you manage to look so calm onstage?" Crystal asked.

Jacey thought for a moment. "I guess, backstage, in this room, I obsessed over being voted out, and disappointing everyone: my parents, my friends, my school, every viewer who'd voted for me. But then I got into character as soon as I got onstage. I became someone else, not Jacey the contestant. Does that make sense?"

It didn't, really. Not to Crystal, P.J., or Todd, judging by their puzzled expressions. Only Garrett, the quiet guy at the end of the couch, nodded.

"So, c'mon, guys," coaxed Desi, warming up to her self-appointed role as MC. "You're going out there soon— don't you want to know anything else?"

"How much money do you make?" asked Crystal, her eyes glittering.

Jacey did a double take, not expecting that question.

"Jacey has no idea how much money she makes. She's got people who stay up all night counting it for her," Desi deadpanned.

"Really?" Crystal's jaw dropped.

And she's stupid, too, Jacey caught herself thinking. Just what showbiz needs, another dumb-bunny starlet.

Desi's comment elicited a grin from sandy-haired Garrett, who'd been silent so far: a grin that lit up his entire face. Jacey smiled back at him.

"Have you met a lot of stars?" P.J. asked breathlessly.

"Are the clubs as cool as they look?" Todd wanted to know.

"Have you ever partied with Lindsay Lohan?" asked Crystal.

Just then, the door to the dressing room was flung open, followed by a booming voice. "I *heard* a rumor a certain winner from last year was here! Are you too famous to come say hi to your old friends, the judges?"

Jacey spun around and saw that the always boisterous, often flamboyant Alex Treadwell had barged into the dressing room. Spiky-haired, pudgy Alex, wearing his usual loud *That '70s Show* plaid vest, was a former child star and current Hollywood casting agent. Despite his over-the-top personality and flamboyant dress code, Alex took his judging job seriously. If he really believed in you, you knew it. Jacey was the contestant he'd believed in most the year before.

"Alex! It's so great to see you!" Jacey ran to embrace him.

"And what am I?" chimed another sonorous voice. "Shredded kibble and bits?" Lean, ponytailed Lloyd Werber, famous for directing teen horror movies, had followed Alex into the room.

"What was all that screaming I heard before?" Lloyd asked, "I was about to call nine-one-one."

"Crystal and P.J. came a little unglued when they met Jacey," Desi explained.

"I have no idea why," Jacey said modestly.

"Are you kidding me?" Alex asked. "They came unglued because you're living proof that this show discovers real talent. If you could do it, so can any one of them."

Well, maybe not *any* one of them, Jacey thought an hour later as she watched the first pair of contestants act out their scene. She was on the panel, seated at Alex's left. Lloyd was on his right, and Miss Sabrina, a former drama teacher, was seated next to him.

She was the judge all the contestants had had the most trouble with. Miss Sabrina wasn't as droll as Lloyd, and she didn't gush like Alex. Few even understood what she was saying. It was surprising to see her back.

Judge Jacey now focused on the pair of actors onstage. Tiny P.J., overshadowed in every way by Todd, was doing a yellow-brick-road scene from *The Wizard of Oz*. Todd was playing the cowardly lion to P.J.'s spunky Dorothy. They didn't suck. P.J. came out of her shell, while gregarious Todd relayed cowardice by retreating into one of his own.

Jacey's instant assessment: they'd picked the wrong characters and the wrong scene in the wrong movie. They weren't playing on their strengths.

When they were done, however, the studio audience went wild! Waving signs declaring their loyalty either to P.J.'s peeps or "Hot Rod" Todd, they were on their feet, hooting and clapping.

Alex passed Jacey a note: *Look at this audience. You'd think Judy Garland and Burt Lancaster came back from the dead for one more take.*

Jacey burst out laughing. She elbowed Alex and whispered, "You're a bad, bad lad! But . . . spot-on." She was interested in seeing what Alex would actually say to the twosome once the cameras were on him.

The former kid star lit up and went into gush mode: "Oh, my God, you did *The Wizard of Oz*. My favorite movie!" He addressed P.J.: "Darling, you brought spirit to Dorothy. I kept wishing we'd see you fall into the poppy field.

"And Todd, I love that you used your leonine head of scarlet hair to show us the Cowardly Lion. Such a brave decision!"

Lloyd, the director, disagreed vehemently. "You should have tried the Tin Man," he said to Todd. "At least you would have been believable. And P.J., sorry, I didn't see the fear in Dorothy's eyes—in fact, with your bangs so long, I didn't see her eyes at all. You'd have made a more convincing Toto."

Was Jacey the only one to see the tears well up in P.J.'s eyes?

Miss Sabrina felt they ought to have "elucidated, dears, used your bodies to express yourselves, jump into those lines with more passion!" Was she deliberately pronouncing Todd as "Toad"?

Then it was Jacey's turn. She aimed for helpful but made it only as far as lame. "I'm wondering"—she put her finger to her chin—"if doing this movie wouldn't have been more *fun* if Todd had been the Wizard to P.J.'s Dorothy. Play up your um . . . physical . . . differences."

Jacey vowed to do better with the next pair.

Garrett and Crystal acted out a classic scene from the

romantic comedy *Pretty Woman*. Something told Jacey this had been Crystal's idea. When their turn was up, the Club Crystal cheerleaders cried out, "Crystal Sparkles!" and "Go, Bleu!" Crystal must've brought all of Toenail, Texas, or wherever she was from, with her. Her crowd was hale and hearty—like her.

By contrast, Garrett's cheering squad was small, but their signs were cool: MCKINLEY = MCWINNER! and MCKINLEY MANIA—LONG MAY IT RULE!

Jacey considered what to say. She went with the truth, accompanied by a bit of self-deprecating humor. "I had trouble believing you two in the Richard Gere and Julia Roberts roles, but at least you had more chemistry than Adam and me in that YouTube scene!"

The judges and the audience howled. Making a joke at her own expense won Jacey points.

It wasn't until each finalist did a solo scene that she screwed up, big-time.

P.J. picked the classic Shakespearean soliloquy *Romeo, Romeo! Wherefore art thou, Romeo?* While the girl made Juliet's despair palpable, Jacey wished she'd chosen a speech that hadn't been done to death.

Crystal took the opposite tack. She came up with something totally original. It was so unfortunate, so giggle-inducing, that Jacey could barely control herself. Crystal tried to act out the words to the Paula Cole song "Bethlehem," about a miserable high school girl in a town bearing a famous biblical name—a town as far from spiritual as you could get. Jacey knew the words well. When you heard it sung, you really felt for the girl. Crystal slaughtered it. For her sake, Jacey hoped few voters knew the song.

Todd went for physical comedy, prancing about in a scene from *Jackass! The Movie*. At least he was trying to be funny, and he got points for that.

It was when Garrett, who'd seemed shy and laid back, came out as Danny Zuko in a tight, white T-shirt with rolled-up sleeves and belted out a song from *Grease* that Jacey totally lost it: the starlet had "chills," and they were multiplyin'.

If only she had kept her chills to herself.

"Oh, my God, he's amazing—he's so hot!" was what she blurted. Her hand flew to her mouth, but it was too late: her mic was on. Every home in America watching *Generation Next* would hear it, and the cameras swiveled quickly to catch her mortified face.

When she sputtered, later on, that it was Garrett's performance that had blown her away, she got more laughs than comedian Todd had.

# Chapter Five

## Gimme Shelter

Red-faced from her *Generation Next* gaffe, Jacey gratefully took off with Desi for Shelter Rock immediately after the taping. Safely inside the limo, she commenced some serious self-hating and texting of apologies to everyone she could think of.

"Enough, Jace," Desi finally said. "Stop whining. And stop texting 'Oops, my bad' to the entire world."

"But no judge ever reacts like that on a reality show. I came off like a starstruck teenybopper," Jacey moaned. "They'll edit it out, right? When the show airs? No one will know?"

"Don't bet on it," Desi said. "They're probably pumped. Your goof-up will make great TV! They might ask you to be a permanent judge, maybe even replace Paula on *American Idol*. Her act is so played. Yours is fresh!"

"It wasn't an act," Jacey sniffed. "I didn't expect him to be so amazing."

"Because *you* haven't been watching all these weeks," Desi said, reprimanding her. "How do you think he made the final four? Well, clearly, the viewers, the actual voters, agree with you. You're the voice of America's heartland."

"I don't think P.J., Todd, or Crystal would be too happy to hear that. They probably hate me. I'm sure Garrett's embarrassed, too." Jacey sulked.

"All right," Desi said. "We're almost there. Time to stop obsessing about your big mistake. Time to meet some people with real problems."

Whoa! Where had that come from? Desi never spoke to her like that. "Jace! I'm so sorry," Desi said, backpedaling. "That came out wrong. Pretend I didn't say it."

"Fine, but riddle me this: what's really up with this Shelter Rock place? Why's it so important to you?"

Desi fixed her gaze somewhere over Jacey's shoulder and mumbled, "You'll see when you get there."

Even hours after the visit, Jacey didn't see what accounted for Desi's passionate persistence.

Shelter Rock looked more like a little house crumbling on the prairie, than a circa-now refuge for kids in crisis.

Situated out in the sticks, surrounded by acres and acres of weeds, Jacey figured it had been a ranch at one time, or a farm maybe. Not that she noticed any animals.

Just outside the clapboard house was a small playground, consisting of a swing set, a slide, and a lone teeter-totter. Little girls played in a sandbox; a bunch of boys hung like monkeys from an ancient jungle gym. Everyone stopped to stare at the shiny limousine that had appeared before them. Yet no one ran over to it.

"They didn't know you were coming," Desi whispered to Jacey. "And, to be honest, I'm not sure that many of them know who you are."

Do they not have TV? Jacey wondered, following Desi into the house.

Jacey and Desi were greeted by Rosalie Cross, who referred to herself as "manager, caretaker, social worker, and mom" to the hundred or so children currently living there. A vibrant middle-aged woman whose colorful style contrasted with the drab surroundings, Rosalie ran Shelter Rock along with a volunteer staff of four and a rotating group of social workers. The kids slept in bunker-like dorm rooms, hung out in a den with two TVs, and took their meals in a large kitchen and dining area. The absence of computers, PlayStations, exercise equipment, or even a single old stereo was painfully obvious to Jacey.

"What about school?" Jacey asked, as they made their way through the hallway toward Ms. Cross's office.

"We bus them to nearby elementary and high schools," Rosalie replied. "Of course, we always have several residents who can't handle traditional school. We tutor them here. Out back are a couple of trailers that we've converted to schoolrooms. Licensed teachers come for three hours a day."

"And you say none of these kids are orphans?" Jacey asked.

"No. They'd be in foster homes," Ms. Cross said. "Shelter Rock was created to be a safe haven for kids who temporarily cannot live with their parents. Families that are in crisis, for one reason or another, have the option of placing a child here—the kids go home eventually. Some stay longer than others."

Admittedly, Jacey had trouble imagining what dire circumstances could force kids into a place like this. Matt's words *Sometimes I forget how sheltered you are* came back to her. But her childhood had had its rough patches. Her dad had taken a hike when she was five, and her mom worked two jobs to support them. It was hard, but Jacey's mom had never thought of turning her out!

The manager finally explained that the property had once been a ranch and had been sold to L.A. County. It had been turned into a shelter for kids in the early 1960s. "However," Ms. Cross said, "it was poorly run and ended up getting a reputation as a juvie jail, filled with problem kids."

"Doesn't look like that now," Jacey remarked. Even though Shelter Rock was definitely run down and badly in need of an upgrade, the kids seemed all right.

The manager smiled broadly for the first time since they'd arrived. "Oh, everything turned around about twelve years ago, when Shelter Rock was turned over to a wonderful, wonderful director. He just got in here, rolled up his sleeves, and worked hard to reunite each and every child with their families. And of course, did his best to make sure their stay here was truly a refuge."

"Sounds like a really cool guy. Have I heard of him?" Jacey asked. She'd attended a bunch of charity bashes recently and met many true philanthropists. That was one of the reasons she'd been inspired to pitch in where she could, too.

Ms. Cross peered down at her hands and fiddled with her bracelets. "I know this will sound odd, but I'd rather not say. He prefers to remain under the radar."

"Why?" Jacey joked. "Is he an ex-con or something?"

"No, nothing like that." The manager shot a furtive look at Desi—a look so fleeting that Jacey might not have noticed it had she not still been trying to figure out Desi's motives—and laughed nervously. "He won't confirm it, but my guess is he must have spent some time here, back when Shelter Rock was—well, to be frank, a hellhole."

"That's probably why he's so dedicated," Desi piped up.

"Absolutely!" Rosalie Cross agreed. "He understands that these kids often fall through the cracks. They're not technically homeless, their problems aren't medical, but their needs are just as great. And Jake—that's what the kids call him—reads to them, plays with them, organizes softball and basketball games, takes small groups for outings. Most importantly, he listens to them. Sure, they need a new playground, new dorms and computers, but they also need to know they haven't been forgotten, and that whatever they're going through at home will pass. They need support."

"He sounds like an amazing person," Jacey remarked.

"He is," Ms. Cross raved, "but there is one thing he *can't* bring to Shelter Rock. He's not a wealthy man and . . ."

Lightbulb. This was where Jacey would come in.

Donating a few hundred thousand dollars would go a long way toward upgrading Shelter Rock.

By the time Jacey and Desi left, it was nearly evening. Jacey hadn't made any commitments to Shelter Rock but apparently hadn't been expected to, either. "We don't want to pressure you," Rosalie had assured Jacey, taking her hand. "We're so grateful you took time from your busy schedule to come visit. It means a lot."

Questions gnawed at Jacey. Why me specifically? she wondered. Why not a more established star, someone with the clout to bring more attention to these children?

The easy answer was sitting right next to her in the backseat of the limo: Desi had contacted them.

The hard question: what was Desi's connection to Shelter Rock?

Matt Canseco took her mind off everything. His Viper was parked in the driveway when she and Des got home, and he was sitting on the living room couch. Jacey catapulted herself into his arms, planting a major mushy kiss on his lips. Only when they pulled apart did she realize that Dash was sitting next to Matt.

Apparently, they'd been playing a video game. "Oops, did I interrupt?" she asked sweetly, batting her eyes at Dash.

"I was just about to kick his butt," her friend grumbled.

Matt joked, "My girl couldn't contain herself—she missed me so much!"

"Always," she murmured, smooching his neck. His girl. Jacey liked the sound of that.

"I called; you didn't pick up," Matt said.

Jacey slid off her boyfriend's lap and checked her cell phone. Sure enough, there were several messages from Maca86. Also from her agent and her publicist.

"It didn't ring," Jacey said. "We must have been out of range."

"In L.A.? I find that hard to fathom," he said, taking her hand.

"Who said anything about being in L.A.?"

"I get it, you bolted way out of town because of that *Generation Next* thing. The blurt that'll be heard round the world when they air it tomorrow night," Matt guessed.

Jacey closed her eyes. "You heard."

"Gossip travels faster than the speed of light in this town," Dash reminded her.

"It's cool, Dimples," Matt assured her. "You're allowed to find other guys hot—just as long as it doesn't go any further than that."

"Jealous?" she asked.

"Me? I don't get jealous. Still, you might want to dial it down next time."

Later, she and Matt sat side by side in a booth at a pizza place in the nearby Malibu Country Mart. They were sharing their "usual" (they already had a usual!), a large pie: half extra cheese, for her; half sausage, for him.

"Maybe one day," Jacey said dreamily, "we'll actually

make a movie together." They'd already come close. Jacey had tried out for and won the lead female role in Matt's movie *Dirt Nap*—only to lose out at the last minute when the producer decided to cast his own daughter instead. There had been nothing Jacey or even Matt could do about it—and the subject remained a sore spot.

"No maybes about it, Dimples," Matt said, "Our turn will come—unless, of course, you'd rather star with Garrett, now that you've seen his acting talent. I don't mind stepping back."

Jacey mock-punched his arm. "Like you're getting away from me that easily! Besides, one stupid slip of the tongue—okay, it was loud and a girl can still hope they don't air it—doesn't mean I want to be in a movie with him."

"If he wins, that'll make twice that the show has given real talent a chance. For reality TV, that blows my mind."

"It'll depend on the voters," Jacey said. "I can see how the other three got to the finals, but Garrett's the real deal."

"If he's such a hot boy wonder, let's hope he doesn't get swallowed up in the Hollywood teen-idol machine."

"Is that what you think happened to me?" Jacey needled him. "That I got caught up in the Hollywood machine?"

"You would have—if I hadn't come to your rescue."

"My hero," she purred, slipping her arm around his waist and moving in for a kiss.

"I have pizza breath," he warned her.

"I am so all about pizza breath," Jacey cooed. Neither noticed the waitress removing their pizza crusts and empty iced tea glasses. They *were* interrupted, however, by—what else?—a paparazzo, whose camera lens was pressed right up against the restaurant window. It took Matt mere seconds to dispatch the intrusive photog, but it didn't matter. The make-out moment was over.

They walked hand in hand along the beach back to the house, stopping every so often for a smooch. The sun had long since gone down, and there was a delicious-smelling breeze coming in from the ocean. Jacey had Matt's hoodie wrapped around her. It kept her warm in every way. Maybe he wouldn't mind, she thought, if she poached it permanently.

They were nearly all the way back home when Matt snapped his fingers. "Almost forgot to tell you—see how you distract me? We just got the premiere date for *Dirt Nap*. It's the Friday after this one."

"So soon?" she asked.

"Yeah, all of a sudden they want to get it out before the end of the year, so it can qualify for awards season."

"Cool!" Jacey exclaimed. "Wait . . . Did you say premiere? Like, the whole red-carpet thing?"

"Nah. It's an indie, remember? Just a few select reporters, the cast and the crew. We'll see the movie and celebrate afterwards."

We. That's what Jacey heard. Had she heard correctly? "Are you, um, inviting me to go with you?"

"You're my chick. Of course you're going." Matt gave her a look that said, *Why would you think otherwise?*

Relieved, she decided to tease him. Just a little. "You sure you want little Miss Wholesome at your dark, twisted indie debut?"

Matt grinned mischievously and bent to pick up a fistful of sand. Before she could react, he rubbed it onto her cheeks. "We'll see if she can't get a little dirty."

Jacey giggled. "Now you'll have to lick it off."

"I was hoping you'd say that."

They were laughing. And kissing. Young lovers with the surf at their feet and the world at their fingertips. Pure bliss. Until Matt's cell phone rang. He checked the caller ID. "Emilio," he said. "I'll call him back later."

Emilio! Jacey couldn't believe she'd forgotten! "Speaking of Emilio, is there a reason you neglected to tell me he's cheating on Ivy?"

Matt looked genuinely puzzled, "Why would I?"

So he did know! "Because he's your best friend, and she's my cousin. He's cheating on her! You don't think that's something I should know?"

Matt drew back. "Maybe you should, and maybe you shouldn't—but either way, it's not my business."

"It kind of is, Matt. You're my boyfriend, and you know I don't want to see her hurt."

"I don't do gossip, I don't do rumors, and unless somebody asks me to get involved in personal matters, I don't. Simple as that." Matt's tone was steady.

"Ivy's my family," Jacey stressed, not comprehending Matt's reasoning. "You should have mentioned it. Let me break it to her."

"Look, Dimples." Matt held his palms up. "I respect your right to handle things your way. You need to respect mine, too."

Jacey crossed her arms over her chest and pouted. Everything had been perfect up till that moment. But this was big. It wasn't some trifle to be excused with "You do things your way, I do them my way."

The next day, Jacey caught Dash in the kitchen brewing an espresso, and she finally talked to him about Ivy. Dash confirmed that it had been Aja who'd confronted Emilio about being with another girl.

"Desi thinks we should tell Ivy," Jacey said thoughtfully. "I'm not sure that's the best idea. What do you think?"

Dash shook his head. "Tough call. Right now, she's completely oblivious. For all we know, it could have been a onetime thing. Aja didn't push him to talk about it."

Even so, shouldn't she know? Jacey wondered. Her instinct told her not to rock the boat until they had more info. Dash agreed. Jacey updated him on the previous day's visit to Shelter Rock. His surprise seemed genuine. He had had no idea that Desi had even checked out a charitable cause, let alone taken Jacey to see the place. Dash was almost ready to talk to Jacey about what he'd researched.

He poured the thick dark liquid into a tiny espresso cup. "So, what do you think? Do you want to make a commitment to Shelter Rock and forget about the other charities?"

"I don't know what I want. There's something *off* about the whole thing. I can't put my finger on it. Can you check it out without Desi knowing? Find out whatever you can—mainly, whether it's on the up-and-up. And while you're at it, see if you can't unearth the mysterious 'Call Me Jake' dude. The one with everything but money."

"I live to serve, O Boss Lady of the 'Bu," Dash said. "Want some coffee?"

"No, but there is one more thing. Block out next Friday on my calendar. It's Matt's *Dirt Nap* premiere."

"No can do. Next Friday's already blocked out."

"For what?"

Dash shook his head in exasperation. "Sweetie, I know we, the posse, exist to take care of these measly details for you, but I should think you'd know when your own red-carpet premiere is."

# jaceyfan blog

## Scoops, Oops, and a Snoopy Question—the Week in Jacey!

Best take cover, Jacey! 'Cause I'm about to *un*cover a whole lotta J-buzz.

**The Big Scoop!** Here's a sneak peek at the dress our starlet will wear on the red carpet at the *Galaxy Rangers* premiere. She's chosen a Posen, that is, a gown by designer to the stars Zac Posen, who has described some of his creations as "fashion-tainment." Jacey's dress is vintage (definition: old-school, like what Great-Granny might've worn), beaded and plunging—perfect for a soiree set in the 1920s, maybe! Too bad her movie is set in the future, not the past!

**The Big Oops!** That'd be her "OMG, he's so hot!" flirty blurt-out to her favorite finalist, Garrett McKinley on *Generation Next*. Everyone laughed at her—everyone except P.J.'s people, that is. Jacey's unkind comments totally got poor P.J. eliminated. How? How about pointing out P.J.'s one tiny goof in her *Romeo and Juliet* soliloquy? So what if P.J. said,

"And I'll be a Capulet no more," instead of "And I'll no longer be a Capulet?" If Jacey hadn't nitpicked, do you really think any voter would have noticed the mistake?

**The Big Snoop!** Don't expect Jacey's shiny new boyfriend, Matt Canseco, to be her date for the *Galaxy Rangers* premiere. Jacey wanted to "come out publicly" as a couple at that event, but it's not gonna happen. Matt doesn't "do" the red carpet—not even for his starlet girlfriend. Piece of advice, Jacey—this "relationship" is headed for disaster. If you're smart, you'll move on. Now would be a good time.

# Chapter Six

## The Red Carpet Rules!
## Too Bad the Movie Doesn't

Maybe Jacey would tire of walking the red carpet one day, and see it as just another boring obligation, like a press conference or an interview. Maybe one day she'd agree with Matt and think the spectacle of bling and beautiful people congratulating each other was obnoxious.

This was not that day.

Call her superficial; color her hypocritical; sometimes, a starlet just can't help herself.

That night's splashy event for *Galaxy Rangers* marked Jacey's third red-carpet appearance. It was a huge rush for her. From the gridlock of limos delivering tricked-out celebrities to the flashbulbs in her eyes and the microphones in her face, the whole scene was magical. In spite of everything she'd seen and learned, when it came to premieres, Jacey Chandliss was a wide-eyed and willing participant.

Not so long ago, she and Desi had totally *lived* for those events—the Emmys, MTV awards, Grammys, Teen Choice Awards, Oscars, Golden Globes—the friends were full-out awards-show gluttons. They'd camp out in Jacey's bedroom, cross-legged on her queen-size bed, eat pizza, and play pint-size critics. Glued to the TV, they'd make snarky or worshipful comments about who wore what and whom showed up with whom. Winners? Losers? Who cared? It was all about who made a fool of herself, forgot to thank her husband, or was clearly sloshed onstage—the Jacey-and-Desi award went to the star who'd given them the most to talk about.

Sure, Jacey and Desi had once fantasized about being there, but much in the same way they had pictured themselves taller, more confident, and more fashionable. Neither girl ever thought it would actually happen. When it did for Jacey, suddenly, swiftly—all except the being-taller part—the celeb swarm-storm that is the red carpet turned out to be even cooler than anything a wishful teen could have conjured up.

Maybe it was the fans behind the ropes, screaming her name, wanting her autograph, a picture, a nod, or a wave;

or the reporters hanging on her every word; perhaps it was her princess-for-a-night ensemble. Okay, so maybe it was the selfish, attention-craving side of Jacey—she'd cop to that. The whole scene was awesome!

Even if the hoopla was for a movie that everyone knew was a bomb. This was the pre-screening lovefest; a whirlwind of good wishes and gushy kisses before the post-screening reality-calamity set in.

Even if her date was Ivy instead of Matt. Jacey had chosen Ivy for the spotlight position because she felt sorry for her cousin, and guilty for remaining mum about Emilio.

Even if she'd been forced to switch from the beaded, retro dress she craved to a gaudy, ridiculous one—just to foil the blogger! How the he-she monster had gotten a photo of the perfect Zac Posen she'd chosen was a mystery. But no way was she going to prove him-her right.

So, here she was in a high-gloss, metallic, futuristic frock her stylist had chosen. The cocktail-length gown was festooned with rhinestones and, worst of all, had padded, Star Trekian shoulders. Jacey looked more space-tart than film starlet. She'd score on the worst-dressed lists this night.

"Ja-*cey!* I am all about that dress on you!" gushed phonier-than-ever Kate Summers just as Jacey and Ivy hit the red carpet.

Kate was a sister-starlet and full-on frenemy.

"A brave choice for someone so petite!" echoed Kate's shadow, TV actress Sierra Tucson.

Jacey gave good phony, too. "You're rockin' that halter top! Kate—you totally have the body for it." Kate's clothespin shoulders looked ridiculously pointy. To Sierra, Jacey feigned hairdo envy: "I love the crimped-out look—so Christina Aguilera, circa 2005."

Sierra and Kate had no clue they'd been dissed. They beamed.

Jacey's publicist, Peyton, popped up to lead her over to the *Galaxy Rangers* photo op. The studio had trucked in a ginormous prop spaceship for the official cast picture. Like a science-fair class photo, Jacey thought wryly as she took her place between Adam Pratt and Emory Farber.

Adam, preening in a shimmery pale pewter suit, immediately draped an arm around Jacey and planted a kiss on her cheek. That was a bummer; his cologne made her queasy. Emory meanwhile, was visibly shaking. Jacey managed to snake her arm around his prodigious waist. "It's going to be all right, Em," she whispered. "Let's hold our heads up and be proud of the work we did."

Easy for her to say. She already had *Supergirl* lined up.

Jacey's agent, Cinnamon, sleek in Armani, stood off to the side while the photogs snapped away. She was trailed by her assistant, Kia—wearing an ensemble that was best described as vintage dustbin. They made the oddest pair on the red carpet. When the photo op was done, Cinnamon rushed up to Jacey, and not to heap compliments on her star client. "This Garrett kid from *Generation Next*. Ivy insists he's the real deal. Think I should sign him before anyone else does?"

Jacey nodded, giving silent kudos to Ivy. Tipping Cinnamon off showed real initiative; her cousin was catching on fast to the agenting business. Her rise would surely be Kia's downfall, and that couldn't happen soon enough as far as Jacey was concerned. Something about that girl gave her the creeps.

Peyton came to escort Jacey to the press pod, where Joan Rivers, Ryan Seacrest, and the *Entertainment Tonight*, *The Insider*, *Extra*, and *Access Hollywood* hosts waited to talk to her. Jacey managed a brief detour to the roped-off area where hundreds of screaming fans were gathered, hoping for a star-sighting, an autograph, or a picture. Showing them some love, thanking them for coming out to support *Galaxy Rangers* was probably the one genuine thing she would do all night. She scrawled her autograph and posed for as many photos as she could in the short window of time Peyton gave her.

Then it was off to phony-starlet land. She didn't know

which would be worse, having to lie through her teeth about *Galaxy Rangers*, or vague-ing up her personal life.

"Who's your date tonight?" asked *Access Hollywood* after the obligatory prattle about her Viktor & Rolf dress.

"My date is Ivy Langhorne, my junior agent and cousin," Jacey replied proudly.

"Can you confirm that you and Matt Canseco are an item?" chirped the *Insider* guy. Right, like Jacey would give that up without Matt by her side. Expertly masking her disappointment that he wasn't, she goofed on the guy: "An item? Like at the supermarket?"

That stumped, but didn't stop, him. "Is Matt Canseco your boyfriend?"

"He's definitely a boy, and totally a friend. Does that help?" Jacey smiled innocently.

"Why isn't Matt here tonight?" The E! reporter swooped in, piggybacking on the other reporter's interview.

"Matt's incredible new movie, *Dirt Nap*, is also premiering tonight. When you guys are finished here, you should check it out," she said.

*Entertainment Tonight* went for the jugular. "Are you embarrassed about your reaction to Garrett McKinley on *Generation Next*?" he asked smarmily.

*Embarrassed? Why, did I fart?* That's what Desi had told her to say to that inevitable question. Sanity ruled, and she went with the script Peyton had prepared for her: "I wouldn't say embarrassed, it's live reality TV, after all. You never know what'll pop out of your mouth. That's what makes it so much fun for the viewers."

After a few more interviews, robo-Jacey was free to schmooze. She headed straight for the other celebrities. These were her peers now, and she got to chat it up with them, trade air kisses, quasi hugs, and ego-massages. Major movie stars like Charlize and Scarlett had arrived with their entourages. Lindsay brought her sister and brother, since *Galaxy Rangers* was a family movie, after all. Jacey had face time with Justin, Jessica, Kelly, an Olsen twin (Jacey still couldn't tell which was which) and a coterie of *High School Musical* cuties.

She totally knew that these brief conversations were insincere at best—but she admitted, proudly even, that this was fun for her. She was the one being watched on TV now, being talked about by young fans; she was the star many dreamed of becoming.

It was cool to feel like part of a community. There were moments when only a sister-starlet, or fellow thespian, could really understand what you were going through. Actors "got" each other. That was what made dating come naturally. Showbiz couples worked, as long as the rivalry thing didn't *become* a thing. Luckily, that would never happen with her and Matt.

A beaming, superslinky Ivy sidled up to Jacey and linked arms with her. "I totally owe you for telling Cinnamon I was right about Garrett. She's really impressed with me."

"You're doing great—I'm proud of you," Jacey said.

"How 'bout we celebrate after the screening?" Ivy suggested. "Instead of going to the *Galaxy* afterparty, why don't we go see Matt and Emilio?"

Jacey froze. Could Ivy hear her heart racing? Did guilt give off a vibe?

She stammered, "Mmmm . . . not sure, Ives. Wouldn't it look bad for the star to skip out on her own afterparty?"

"You did your civic celebri-duty to Avalon Studios, the cast, director, agent, and publicist. As your almost–junior agent and blood relative, I hereby release you from *Galaxy* prison!" Ivy said breezily.

Jacey hesitated.

"Besides," Ivy continued, "the afterparty won't miss you too much. It's for the entire cast and crew. If anyone says anything, I'll make up an excuse. I'll say you suddenly got cramps and I had to take you home. Whatcha say?"

Jacey's heart leaped; it said, *Oh, yeah! A chance to*

*see Matt tonight? Tasty.* Her head said, *Uh-oh. Ivy cannot go if Emilio is there with . . . whoever that person is. That cannot happen.*

Jacey spent most of the screening texting back and forth with Matt, who was in the middle of his own screening in a different theater.

*Howzit going?* she asked him.

*Good,* he responded. *So far. U?*

Jacey looked up at the movie screen, and her stomach sank. The scene foreshadowing her character's kiss with Adam was playing. The kiss leaked on YouTube had stayed in the picture after all.

*Not so great,* she responded.

*Ur being overcritical,* he wrote back kindly.

She looked up at the screen again, only to see herself and Adam "flying" through the galaxy, arguing while on patrol. No-o-o-o . . . She was probably being undercritical.

Ivy elbowed her. "What are you doing?" she whispered.

"Texting Matt."

"Ask him where the afterparty is, but don't mention me. I want to surprise Emilio."

Jacey's spirits were sinking fast. It was official: her movie sucked. And Ivy was going to insist on going to Matt's afterparty.

Jacey decided to go for the misery trifecta. She asked

Matt about the girl who'd stolen her part. *Is she any good?*

Matt took his time answering that one. Finally, he wrote: *U would have been better.*

Who said Matt couldn't be diplomatic—or outright lie to protect her feelings? He really was the best boyfriend. Suddenly, Jacey ached to see him, to hold him, to thank him—for being him. She snuck a sidelong glance at Ivy. Her cousin's eyes were on the screen, but she was biting her lip: a telltale sign that she, too, was unthrilled with the movie.

Jacey felt a twinge of guilt. Ivy would tell her the truth. That was what a loyal friend did. Whereas, for the past several weeks, she'd been totally lying to Ivy, by omission.

She quickly texted Matt again: *Ivy wants to come to your afterparty. Is it safe?*

Again, Matt didn't reply instantly. Eventually, he wrote that the party would be at Dungeon, his favorite out-of-paparazzi-range dive bar, and urged her to show up. He didn't respond to her query. It occurred to her that perhaps he hadn't understood it. Only later would she think he actually had.

# Chapter Seven

## Averting Double-D Disaster

Jacey and Ivy snuck out before the closing credits. That way, the starlet avoided having to plaster on a smile and gush about how great the movie had turned out. She did not have an ounce of phony left in her.

As the limo sped them across town to the *Dirt Nap* afterparty, Jacey remarked, "This feels *so* junior high, sneaking off to the bad-boy party instead of attending our own G-rated gala. Maybe we shouldn't."

"Oh, come on!" Ivy waved dismissively. "How much more time did you want to spend with Adam, Kate, and Sierra all saying how great the movie was? Desi will represent for us tonight. We're going to have fun—we both deserve it!"

*Tell her now!* Jacey's conscience pricked her. *You can't let her be blindsided. She'd hate you forever, and she'd be right!* Only . . . Jacey didn't know for sure that Emilio would be there, let alone his hook-up. How much would it suck to tell Ivy something she didn't need to know?

"Stop biting your nails!" Ivy scolded her. "You're chewing away close to a hundred dollars there!"

Jacey looked down. She hadn't even realized she'd been doing it. "Maybe we should go home and change first. And I can get a quick touch-up to fix this," she suggested.

*Maybe I can call Matt without her hearing, and find out for sure about Emilio,* she thought.

"Matt will be so psyched to see you he won't care that you look like a nail-biting Seven of Nine," Ivy said.

Jacey elbowed her sharply in the ribs. "Now you tell me I look ridiculous? Way to be honest, Cuz!"

"Lighten up, Jacey! You insisted on proving blogger-boy wrong at the last minute. This was the best your stylist could do under the circumstances. Anyway, the dress worked for the red carpet. You looked like . . ."

". . . I was sent from another galaxy?"

Ivy leaned over and fluffed the winged shoulders of Jacey's dress. "Let's leave the trash talk for Cojo and the fashion police."

"They should thank me for giving them so much to make fun of," Jacey grumbled.

"Even more reason to split," Ivy said. "Anyway, schlepping back to Malibu will take too long. By the time we get to Dungeon, Matt and Emilio will be long gone."

If only—Jacey thought.

The cousins arrived just as the *Dirt Nap* party was getting started. At her own high-heeled peril, Jacey bolted down the stairs so she could scope out the scene before Ivy did. The music was blasting, and the dark bar was jam-packed. In contrast to the glammed-up VIPs at Jacey's premiere, the revelers here were grunged down, as if guests had taken the film's title for their dress code cues.

Matt saw her immediately. How could he not, when her dress stood out like a radiating satellite dish against a starless black sky? As Ivy had predicted, Matt was so pumped to see Jacey that he didn't even comment on her ridiculous ensemble. "Dimples! You made it!" He drew her toward him for a serious smooch.

"Where's Emilio?" Jacey asked. In midkiss, it came out sounding like *Mwweees me-lo?*

"Huh?" Matt's dark eyes sparkled. *His* screening must have gone phenomenally well.

Ivy reached them and congratulated Matt. She had

just started to ask about Emilio when they were joined by Dash, Aja, Matt's friend Rob, and some others Jacey didn't recognize. Everyone was raving about the movie and asking how *Galaxy Rangers* had done. As Ivy fielded the questions, Jacey slipped her hand into Aja's and backed away from the circle. "Is he here? With her?" she asked frantically.

The tall, gawky boy nodded grimly and gestured toward the bar. Emilio, easily recognizable by his shoulder-length white-blond hair, was getting drinks and gabbing. Jacey made straight for him. She was about to tap him on the shoulder and let him know Ivy was there, when he spun around, his face registering surprise at the sight of her. He was clutching two drinks: a beer for himself and a flute of pink champagne. Translation: *she* was there. Who else would the girly bubbly be for?

Jacey never got a chance to talk to Emilio. Ivy had found them, and she jubilantly greeted her erstwhile boyfriend. "Emilio! There you are! And you got me a drink already? That's so sweet!" In her four-inch heels and slinky, jade-colored, floor-length gown, Ivy towered over Emilio, a sparkling princess to his ragged-jeans pauper. She blithely plucked the champagne flute out of his hand and took a sip. "Mmmm, this is sweet." Her eyes twinkled. "So, Matt told you? I wanted to surprise you!"

"It's a total surprise," Emilio confessed.

That's probably the only truthful thing he's told her in a long time, Jacey thought.

"Well, come on," Ivy urged after downing her drink. "Let's get on the dance floor. I'm ready to party!" Before Emilio could protest, Ivy was leading him into the crush of dancers.

Meanwhile, Matt found his way over to Jacey. He draped an arm around her and nuzzled her neck. "How'd you manage to escape the *Galaxy* affair?"

But he didn't give her time to answer. His lips were on hers, and she responded. When it came to Matt Canseco, her body didn't always follow her brain's directions. They kissed as if they were the only people in the room. Oh, how Jacey did not want to pull away. She had to, though.

"Ivy's here!" She finally blurted out when they came up for air.

"I know," Matt said with a grin. "I see her on the dance floor, shakin' her groove thing."

"What about Emilio's hook-up? Is she here?" Jacey's voice was low, urgent.

Matt shrugged. "Don't know. I have a few other things on my mind tonight besides the tawdry sex lives of our friends. Like, my movie!"

Jacey had never seen Matt that thrilled. He was

practically oozing satisfaction and joy. Making movies he was passionate about, movies that mattered, was what brought him pure happiness, Jacey thought. This, tonight, was his bliss. There was no way Jacey was going to ruin it. Besides—she snuck a glance at the dance floor—Ivy appeared safe for the moment. She and Emilio were gyrating, laughing, and dancing as if neither had a care in the world.

Jacey turned her full attention to her boyfriend, favoring him with her sweetest smile. "So, it went really well?"

"Just the way I hoped," Matt confirmed. "Man, was I relieved."

"You were nervous?"

"You always have doubts at the last minute," Matt said. "What if I'd been wrong about the whole thing? What if it was really crap?"

Matt's vulnerability was so sweet.

"I don't care if the movie earns one buck or one billion," Matt went on earnestly. "I just hope it makes people think. That's all I really want."

The R-rated *Dirt Nap*, with its dark themes of deception and betrayal, would play in a few select theaters, in a few big cities. It was meant for an intelligent audience, the kind of audience that sought out smaller, arty films—as opposed to her own popcorn fest, which would open in every multiplex in the country.

Jacey wanted to feel nothing but happiness for Matt. What did it say about her, then, that the longer Matt went on about his triumph the harder it was for her to quash her jealousy—and her growing resentment? *She* should have been part of that movie; *she* should have costarred as the complex, manipulative character Sarah. *She* should have been sharing the spotlight alongside Matt, instead of making do with the role of adoring starlet girlfriend of megatalented, multifaceted actor.

It wasn't just envy gnawing at her. It was the principle of the thing. He got to make the movies he wanted to. She made the movies she was told to make.

"I'm just so damned proud of the film," Matt crowed.

*Wish I could say the same.* Instantly, Jacey kicked herself—way to be supportive, selfish starlet! She slipped her arm around his waist. "Let me buy you a drink. I'm so proud of you, so pumped that you stuck to your guns and made the movie you wanted to."

Was that a tear in the corner of Matt's eye? He hugged her. "I can't get close enough to you," he murmured. "This dress is like a chastity fortress."

"I know, I hate it," she giggled. "I can't wait to get out of it."

"I can help with that," he said with a sly wink.

"The sooner the better," she whispered.

"You're tempting me, Dimples."

"Isn't that my job as your official girlfriend?" she asked playfully.

"I can't wait for you to see the mov—" Matt started to say. He stopped himself. "If you can't do it, it's cool."

"I'm totally over losing the part!" Jacey lied. "Just stick to your story about the producer's daughter-dearest being awful."

"She nearly sank the movie," Matt confirmed. "They had to pay for an acting coach, and a dialect coach to stay on the set with her. They practically had to draw *X*s on the ground so she'd remember where to stand in each scene."

That shouldn't have made Jacey smirk. But it did.

A group of people had made their way over to them— to Matt, that is. The director of *Dirt Nap*, Noel Langer, and several producers Jacey remembered from her own audition, came over, smiling. All were toasting Matt, fawning over him, lauding his fine performance. Jacey felt invisible.

"You made me look good." Noel Langer clapped Matt on the back.

"Today's indie star, tomorrow's Johnny Depp," crowed the producer Jacey had privately nicknamed Scowly at her audition.

"Next year's Oscar, that's what I'm counting on!" raved another producer, who was puffing on a cigar.

"You guys are getting ahead of yourselves," Matt said modestly.

"And let's not forget the beautiful job my daughter did," bragged Scowly. "You taught her so much!"

Jacey managed to smile through gritted teeth. *She should get an Oscar just for this performance!*

Right on cue, daughter dearest—or Double D's—as Jacey instantly dubbed her, materialized. She wore tacky booty-call shorts and a cropped pink top so tight it left little to the imagination. She did a poor imitation of Jessica Simpson as Daisy Duke as she sipped her drink and said, "Hi, Daddy. Are you having a good time?"

Someone tapped Jacey on the shoulder, and she spun around. Aja. He nodded solemnly toward Double D's. "That's her," he whispered in Jacey's ear.

"I know!" Jacey whispered back. "The skank who stole my role."

Aja arched his eyebrows. "I *mean*," he said pointedly, "that's *her*."

Jacey's jaw dropped. No way. Double D's was Emilio's hook-up?

"What's going on? What are you two whispering about?" Matt asked.

"Her!" Jacey said indignantly, "What's she—"

"Oh. DeeDee Thorne *is* in the movie, Dimples," Matt

said gently. "She kinda has to be here. Unfortunately."

"She's with Emilio!" Jacey felt herself start to quake with rage. Matt knew Jacey resented DeeDee—who had obviously met Emilio through him! *That* was why Matt refused to get involved.

"Hey, Matteo," DeeDee said, striding right up to them. Her boobs were practically in Jacey's face. "Where'd my Emilio go?"

*Matteo? My Emilio?* Just who did this role-and-boyfriend-robber think she was?

DeeDee peered down her ski-slope nose at Jacey. "Oh, hi, aren't you Jancee, or Joycey?" She made it sound like *Joi-zee*.

"This is Jacey Chandliss," Matt said, correcting her. "She's an actress." He emphasized the last word, and his meaning was clear: *as opposed to you, who got the role through nepotism.*

"Whatever." DeeDee shrugged and scanned the room. "Oh, there he is. I almost didn't see him—that green giraffe he's dancing with is hiding him."

DeeDee made a move toward the dance floor, but Jacey latched on to her arm. "You don't wanna do that," she seethed. "Emilio's with his girlfriend now."

"Really?" DeeDee smirked. "Let's go see if he got that memo."

Jacey was about to stop her again when Matt took her by the shoulders. "Let it go; don't get involved."

"Don't . . . ?" she sputtered. "Ivy's my—"

"Mind your business. It's their drama, not yours."

What was he saying? *Don't ruin my night? Don't make a scene? Don't let sympathy for your cousin screw with my happiness?*

Jacey tried to swallow her fury but couldn't. Ignoring Matt, she kicked off her silver Roger Vivier high-heeled shoes and raced through the crowd. She reached Ivy a second before Double D's did. Panting, she spun Ivy around and grabbed her hands. "Come with me! It's . . . it's . . . a crisis!"

Miraculously, Jacey got Ivy out of the way before Double D's could do any damage. Dash and Aja, alert to impending disaster, rallied and somehow managed to block Ivy from seeing her rival pour herself into Emilio's arms.

"What's the matter? What's going on?" a very confused Ivy asked. "Why are the three of you acting so weird?"

Jacey shepherded Ivy into the ladies' room while debating exactly what to say. Would she tell her now and cause a scene? Not say anything and just get her out of there? Jacey opted for the easy way out—she faked major nausea.

Ivy was suspicious. "You were fine two minutes ago; what happened?"

Good thing Jacey was an actress, and a damned good one. She gripped her stomach and closed her eyes. "Ives . . . I'm going to hurl. I need air. Please, get me out of here."

"You didn't even drink or have anything to eat, how could—?"

"—I did have a drink," Jacey croaked. "It's coming up—hurry!"

# jaceyfan blog

## Jeers for Jacey's Movie—
## Cheers for Matt's!

Can you smell it? Pee-eeww! The stench of the reviews for Jacey's latest movie is stinking up the *Galaxy!* The movie was unanimously booed by every critic forced to sit through it. Did our heroine know it was that bad? Jacey, who will pocket a cool six million—that's dollars, people—for her "work" in *Galaxy Rangers*, couldn't even be bothered to stay at the premiere long enough for the credits to roll! According to my eyewitness sources, Jacey pulled a fast one. She escaped the afterparty, where reporters waited, and darted over to boyfriend Matt Canseco's fiesta instead.

Speaking of, *Dirt Nap*'s reviews blew away all the competition. Matt's movie was as widely praised as Jacey's was panned. Will this lead to more trouble in paradise? Or was that already brewing, due to Jacey's obvious attraction for a certain *Generation Next* contestant? Fasten your seat belts, Jacey fans. We feel a rumbling on the way.

# Chapter Eight

## The Field Trip

"You should sue them!" *Generation Next* contestant Crystal Bleu, palming a mirror and applying lip gloss, huffed as she settled into the plush backseat of the Town Car. "Don't let them get away with trash-talking you!"

"Yeah," Todd agreed, planting himself next to her. "You should dig up dirt on them, then spread it around."

Jacey and Ivy were sitting on the jump seats of the car facing them. They were taking the three finalists on a field trip—a gimmick dreamed up by the *Generation Next* execs to show them a day in the life of Jacey Chandliss. Which would, of course, be filmed for a DVD bonus.

Crystal and Todd were dreaming up revenge fantasies on Jacey's behalf. Even if the two high school graduates weren't as smart as your average fifth grader—or starlet.

"It's freedom of the press. It's the reviewers' jobs to write their opinions of the movie," Garrett offered softly, sliding in next to Todd. "But the way they wrote it—you can tell they enjoyed ripping *Galaxy Rangers* to shreds."

"You put that very diplomatically, Garrett," Ivy said.

A blush crept up Garrett's neck, and his gaze dropped to his scuffed hiking boots.

Jacey planted her elbows on her knees and leaned toward the trio. "I'm supposed to be showing you guys what it's really like for a young star in this town. So here goes: bad reviews suck. But you can't let them get to you. Unless the critic writes something you can actually learn from, you *have* to let it roll."

"And cry all the way to the bank," Crystal sniffed. "You'll probably make more from that movie than any of those jerks will ever see in their whole lives." She jingled her bangles for effect.

"Jacey doesn't think that way," Ivy put in quickly. "Like all serious actors, she tries to choose parts she really loves, or do movies she hopes will entertain people."

Nice save! Jacey had to give her cousin props. Between them, they'd just told two lies within the first two minutes of the day! How very Hollywood.

She had picked *Galaxy* at least partly for the big pay-check. The reviews *had* stung. But the kids didn't need to know any of that. They looked up to her.

Now, as she regarded them—eager beaver Todd, clad in khakis and polo shirt; tarted-up Crystal in a dress so short and tight Jacey could only hope she wasn't planning a Britney-style commando exit from the limo; and Garrett, the hot, thoughtful, Bon Jovi look-alike. Next year, one of them would be showing someone else the Hollywood ropes. It boggled her mind.

"It has to give you some satisfaction," Todd was say-ing, "that the movie opened at number one! Just goes to show, critics are bogus. The fans came to see it."

That made Jacey feel worse. She hadn't given her fans what they deserved—a stellar performance in a good movie. This was something else she wasn't sharing with the hopeful threesome facing her. Nor would she share the fact that *Galaxy Rangers'* box-office status would plummet the following week and be out on DVD before the year's end.

"We all feel good about the fan support," Ivy finally said to Todd.

"But . . ." Garrett said, "isn't it one thing when review-ers criticize your movie and another when they rag on you personally?"

Jacey looked up at him. His cornflower blue eyes were ringed by unexpectedly dark lashes. Under her stare, he smiled and blushed slightly. She liked his smile, she decided. It was unaffected . . . and . . . what? Not jaded. He wasn't trying to be clever, or ironic. How refreshing!

"That's a really good point, Garrett," she conceded. "A lot of reporters mix up the two things. Personal attacks are something you have to be ready for."

"How?" Garrett asked. "How can anyone possibly get ready for that?"

Roughly twenty minutes later, they glided through the massive gates of Avalon Studios. Jacey observed the faces of her guests as they gazed intently through the tinted windows of the Town Car. Her first time on a real studio lot had been like winning a golden ticket to a magical wonderland—a universe where imagination and creativity ruled, a universe that wasn't open to the public. All who entered had a part to play there.

They wove through the narrow streets and alleyways of the mazelike studio lot, passing dozens of soundstages. To an outsider—or, in showbiz-speak, a nonpro (Dash liked to joke, "In this town, they call a brain surgeon a nonpro!")—the soundstages looked like warehouses: wide, windowless, hangar-sized stucco buildings. In the real world, it wouldn't have been surprising to find an assembly-line plant inside one, a storage facility inside another. A TV show or major motion picture was being filmed in each of these buildings. Fictional worlds had been constructed in these soundstages, everything from the halls of *Hannah Montana*'s school to the *CSI* labs. The fact that you could walk off a street like that right into the *Grey's Anatomy* operating room or find yourself on the *Star Wars* planet Tatooine always filled Jacey with awe. She never failed to get excited on a studio lot. It was the same tingling anticipation shopaholics got when they crossed the threshold into a new boutique, or that book-lovers felt when they opened a new tome: so many possibilities, so much potential for pleasure!

Garrett's wide eyes and slack jaw signaled his immediate entrancement—but Todd and Crystal, who weren't feeling it the way Jacey was, simply craned their necks looking for stars.

They got excited only when Ivy informed them that the massive trailers parked outside the soundstages might be stars' dressing rooms. Crystal squinted, trying to read the names taped to the doors. "Oooh, I think that one said, 'Drake Bell'!" she shouted. "He's so yummy!"

Todd nearly leaped over Garrett attempting to get out of the car when Ivy remarked, "I think this is where they do the TV show *Heroes*." Todd was all about the cheerleader. "She is smokin'! If she's here, I'm meeting her, dude!"

Jacey chuckled to herself. Being this starstruck was one thing when you were a fan, a nonpro—but something else for a fellow actor (as one of these three, apparently, would soon become). They'd learn. She had.

The limo pulled on to what appeared to be a small-town street, scattered with wooden frame houses and lined with tall, sturdy oak trees.

"People live here?" asked clueless Crystal.

"They aren't real," Ivy explained. "They're just facades, the outsides of houses. This is one of the sets for Jacey's next movie, *The Return of Supergirl*."

Garrett started to open the car door, but Crystal reached over Todd to grab his arm. "Don't!" she admonished him. "Wait for the chauffeur to open it. That's what you do, right, Jacey?"

Jacey shrugged. "Really, either way is okay."

The group was met by one of the ADs (assistant directors) assigned to give them a VIP tour. Since production for *Supergirl* had just begun, most of the sets were under construction, he explained, leading them toward the house that Jacey's character, Linda Danvers, "lived" in.

"Do they know who else is in the cast?" Todd asked the AD.

"Why, are you vying for Jimmy Olsen?" Crystal nudged him.

"If I win, I get to be in some movie—why not *Supergirl*?" Todd replied.

Jacey hung back, opting out of the tour. She'd be spending plenty of time on this "street" when filming actually started. She wanted to check her messages.

Matt had tried to contact her several times that day, she noted. He had been ultrasupportive since she'd been savaged for *Galaxy Rangers*. Killing her with kindness—wasn't that the expression?

Jacey chastised herself for even thinking that. It was just . . . the whole situation sucked. It'd been bad luck that their movies had opened the same weekend and that the reviews had come out simultaneously.

While her major motion picture was being jeered at, his edgy little indie was being universally cheered, hailed as the next *Godfather*! As in, four-star ratings, A+ grades, and reviews that raved: *If you see only one movie this year, make it* Dirt Nap. *You'll be shocked, intrigued, and strangely moved by this under-the-radar film. Matt Canseco gives the performance of the year. Can Oscar afford to snub this one?*

The reviews for Jacey's movie, gleefully exposed by the blogger, were summed up by the current week's *Time* magazine: *Flee the galaxy if you must, but avoid* Galaxy Rangers *at all cost.* No stars, D+ rating. And, in one of the kinder musings: *Chandliss Listliss: Jacey sleepwalks through this movie.*

Since everyone knew that Jacey and Matt were a two-some, someone was bound to give voice to the obvious: love him; hate her. Matt wore the talent in the relation-ship; she was the one-hit wonder. He had star power; she was a mere starlet.

Matt was too smart and too kind to think that. But Jacey was neither. Bad reviews didn't just hurt a relation-ship, in her opinion. They could kill it. If you let them.

*If you let them.* That was what she kept telling her-self.

"The choice is yours, Jace-face," Dash had said the day before. "You can be destroyed by your self-doubts or choose to believe in yourself."

"You've got a great career as a cliché inventor," Jacey had sniffed uncharitably. But Dash knew her well and loved her deeply; he wasn't insulted or thrown off base.

"What did Matt tell you?" He'd coaxed her: "Come on, repeat it. I insist."

What Matt had said—texted, IM'd, emailed—was this: *The most gifted musicians release stinker CDs; not every picture an artist paints is a masterpiece—and all actors make dumb-ass choices sometimes. People forget. You should, too. Today's reviews were tomorrow's "so five minutes ago."*

Easy for him to say, she'd pouted. Had Matt ever gotten a bad review in his life? She thought not.

Her phone rang, jolting her out of her negativity. "How goes it with the *Gen Next* wannabes?" Matt asked. "Do you need rescuing? Should I swing by and kidnap you?"

A week ago, she would have swooned at that suggestion—maybe even found a way to make it work. But today, her reply was terse, and tinged with bitterness. "I can't just leave. I do have responsibilities."

Silence. Jacey felt ashamed. Why was she acting like a bratty ingrate, as if this were all his fault? "I'm sorry," she mumbled. "I didn't mean that like it sounded. See you later?"

"Sure, Dimples," Matt said tonelessly, before hanging up.

Ivy and the *Generation Next*-ers were exiting the set now, and Jacey went over to join them. Garrett and the AD were having an animated conversation, while Todd and Crystal looked like bored schoolchildren, dragged along on a yawn-inducing museum visit.

This attitude, Ivy explained later to Jacey, was the result of getting up close to the less-than-glam aspect of being a movie star. The AD had described the technical stuff that went into a major production. It wasn't exciting, and there weren't any stars around, just regular people: carpenters, electricians, camerapeople—the crew, in short, doing their jobs. It was just like real life—exactly what Todd and Crystal had hoped to escape by winning on *Gen Next*.

Neither a cruise through the wardrobe department nor a tour of the hair and makeup trailer was going to be more exciting for Crystal or Todd than any of the rest of it, so Jacey told the AD that they were going to skip that and go straight to lunch.

Jacey led the group to the commissary, the studio's restaurant–cum–snack bar. Maybe, if they were lucky, she stage-whispered to Ivy, a random actor would be chowing down. "Maybe even . . . oooh, the cheerleader!"

Ivy shot Jacey a "don't be jaded" look.

Crystal had assumed that the word *commissary* meant "chic eatery," so she pulled a face when she saw that the showbiz translation was "cafeteria." As in, pick up a tray, get on line, and tell the nice people behind the counter what you want.

"I thought we were going someplace cool!" Crystal, who hadn't removed her dark designer sunglasses, whined.

"This is cool," said Garrett, checking the place out.

"No, it isn't. It's ordinary." Todd crossed his arms. "We have cafeterias at school!"

Garrett laughed and tucked his longish hair behind his ears. "That's the point. When you're an actor, this is part of your . . . I don't know . . . ordinary life." He looked at Jacey and Ivy. "That didn't come out right, but you know what I mean."

"No, that's it, exactly," Jacey started to agree when she caught Crystal rolling her eyes at Todd. Uh-oh, did it look as if she were favoring Garrett? Again? "We could go somewhere else," she offered.

"Just know that whoever wins *Generation Next* and gets a part in a movie *will* be eating right here," Ivy said, heading toward the food line.

Crystal followed reluctantly. "So you're saying the stars eat here, too? Like George Clooney—and Drake Bell?"

Putting those two actors in the same sentence was enough to stun Jacey—whose only thought was: *please, America, do not let this girl win.*

Ivy didn't skip a beat. "Hey, if Mr. Clooney were making a movie here, I'm sure he'd come over to grab a bite."

Crystal looked around. For a second, Jacey almost wished she could produce Drake . . . whatever his name was. Or the cheerleader, for Todd.

After lunch, Jacey and Ivy made an executive

decision: ditch the *real* in "reality of a working actor's life" for pure fantasy.

In other words, the fun stuff that being a star got you. Such as . . . shopping!

The *Generation Next* execs had given Ivy a credit card, which was burning a hole in her Prada pouch.

Predictably, Crystal's and Todd's moods improved when Ivy informed them that they were headed for a shop-a-thon on Melrose Avenue, the street where celebrity-populated boutiques were lined up like limos on Academy Awards night.

They went to edgy shops like Necromance (for skull-and-crossbones accessories) and Wasteland (ultrahip retro clothes), and they mixed it up at the most famous shop in L.A.: Ron Herman at Fred Segal, which stretched over an entire block.

Score! Crystal was dazzled! These were the boutiques the stars flocked to! She'd read all about them in *Us Weekly* and *In Touch*.

Todd was all over the men's department at Fred Segal. Especially after Ivy said, "They sell Hilfiger and Nautica bathing trunks (for later, when we hang out at Jacey's beach house)."

*My beach house?* Jacey mouthed to Ivy as Crystal and Todd raced into the stores.

"We have to try harder to show them a good time," Ivy said, now that she was out of Garrett's earshot. "It'll make them feel like stars. Plus, we'll have Desi and Dash to help."

Jacey agreed and called her friends to give them a heads-up. After chatting on the phone, Jacey noticed that Garrett hadn't joined the others. He stood outside Fred Segal, gazing at the windows, hands shoved into the pockets of his no-name jeans.

"Shopping not your thing?" Jacey guessed.

"Not really," he said. "But I don't mind. Everything's so different here—it's all interesting."

"I hope you're not disappointed that we left the studio so quickly," Jacey said. "If you have any questions, anything you want to know, I'm happy to talk."

Garrett seemed uncertain. "I don't want to impose. . . ."

"Go for it," Jacey encouraged him.

Garrett was trying to picture his life, in the event that he won. Not that he was counting on it. "Crystal and Todd come alive for the cameras," he said. "I can see them being really successful in this business."

"Crystal and Todd . . ." Jacey hesitated, choosing her words carefully, ". . . are very popular. They've got a lot of people cheering for them."

Garrett told Jacey that most of his supporters couldn't

afford to come to California to sit in an audience week after week, cheering him on.

"But they're voting by phone and e-mail," Jacey reminded him, "in droves! Or you wouldn't have come this far."

She stopped short of saying how she really felt: *You are so the most talented. Todd is funny—he could be the next David Spade, if he wants it. There's a place for Crystal in Hollywood, too. But you—? You're the whole package.*

If Garrett sussed out her thoughts, he didn't let on. Instead, he opened up about his background and his fears. He was from Narrowsburg, a small town in upstate New York, which, when he and Jacey compared backgrounds, sounded much like Jacey's native Michigan. A lot of what Garrett told her felt familiar.

Garrett McKinley came from a tight, loving, "average" family. He'd caught the acting bug back in grade school, where he played—he blushed recalling it—a pilgrim in the first Thanksgiving. After that, he snared the lead in every play through high school.

Mad acting skills did not make him popular at Narrowsburg Regional High. There, boys did sports, farmed, or hunted. A few were interested in science, or hoped to join the army. The marines, even better.

But drama? Dude, that was just strange.

Garrett—or Gary, as he was called in school—loved nothing more than the challenge of becoming someone else. He studied how Leonardo DiCaprio was different in each role; how Matt Damon could make you believe he was an action hero or romantic rogue. He kept DVDs for weeks, just to study them. His bedroom walls were covered with posters of famous films.

"Mine, too!" exclaimed Jacey. "I was all about the classics. James Dean and Marlon Brando."

Like Jacey, Garrett had a family who supported his love of acting. They paid for acting lessons and drove him hundreds of miles sometimes, just to audition for community theater roles. When *Gen Next* came to New York City, there wasn't even a discussion in their house. The whole family—Garrett had two sisters and a brother—piled in to the van ("So *Little Miss Sunshine*!" Garrett and Jacey both said at once, and laughed) and drove down.

Garrett's unabashed gratitude to and love for his family was written all over his—okay . . . now that Jacey was up close and personal with him, she would admit it—totally swoonworthy face. He really did look just like a younger, more innocent Bon Jovi with his sandy hair and lush lips.

"Jacey? Can I ask you something? If I did win, and they

started writing nasty things about me in the papers, and my parents had to read it . . ."

"You mean, hateful reviews, like the brutal blog?" Jacey cut in.

Garrett smiled ruefully. "It's hard to ignore. I'm not so sure I'd want to put my family through that. What if my sisters got teased in school because of some idiotic thing someone wrote?" Garrett turned a deep shade of red. "I'm sorry, I can't believe I just said that."

"No," Jacey said soberly. "You're smart to consider the whole picture."

Getting trashed and publicly ridiculed was not something you could prepare for. Now, listening to Garrett, Jacey was grateful to be an only child. It'd be a long time before her soon-to-be-born brother was old enough to be teased at school.

Earlier in the week, she had called her parents to warn them about the horrendous *Galaxy Rangers* reviews. "Try not to let it freak you out," she'd instructed.

"Seems like you're upset enough for all of us," her stepdad had said perceptively. "We're fine, just concerned about you."

Jacey's mom, the practical one in the family, mused, "Can you make lemonade?"

Which was Mom's shorthand for: *stop feeling sorry*

*for yourself, and ask: what can I do to turn this into
something positive?*

Nothing! was her knee-jerk, sulky response. Except
that it was her mom asking, and that always forced Jacey
to stop and think. An idea formed. Not brainstorm mat-
erial, but positive nevertheless.

The movie reeked . . . but . . . maybe not in the eyes of
kids. Kids who weren't all Pixar-ed out and jaded, who
didn't spend all day on their PlayStations, Wiis, or iPods.

Kids at Shelter Rock, for instance. Jacey decided to
set up a private screening for them the following week—
how cool would that be? She'd get Dash to charter luxury
buses and Desi to rent out a theater, giving each kid a
VIP pass to the show and a swag bag with gifts afterward.
She and Adam Pratt would host the event and sign
autographs.

Ivy had pressed to call Peyton so that Jacey could get
some positive publicity ("badly needed, I don't have to
remind you," she had reminded her), but Jacey had
refused. Until she figured out what Shelter Rock, and
Desi's involvement in it, was all about, everything stayed
on the d.l. Doing something nice for kids in need felt like
a kind of redemption. That was more than enough for now.

# Chapter Nine

## Jacey [Hearts] Paparazzi

The *Generation Next* finalists headed for the 'Bu, as Ivy had promised. Jacey's cousin played the tour guide role as the limo cruised along the PCH (the Pacific Coast Highway, which winds up the coast of Malibu).

"This is where the Malibu Pier and Surfrider Beach are." Ivy pointed down Sweetwater Canyon Drive. "Lots of movies have used the pier for backdrops. You can catch some of the best waves there."

"When do we get to the really expensive part of Malibu?" asked Crystal. She was eyeing the strips of surf shops and fast-food places as well as the backs of houses so narrow and close together they were practically on top of one another.

"All of it is the expensive part," Jacey told her.

"No way!" Todd didn't believe it. "This looks like . . . Main Street."

"Wait," Ivy said. "It's deceiving. When we pull off the highway, you'll see what's so special about the 'Bu."

Ivy was as good as her word. When they walked through Jacey's house to the beach, Todd and Crystal were both ecstatic.

"This is more like it!" Crystal's eyes lit up.

"Sweet!" said Todd, looking at the gleaming wrap-around deck facing the pristine beach. The aqua-colored ocean, glittering in the late-afternoon sun, was just yards away.

Desi and Dash greeted them with tall, icy drinks, tasty gourmet treats, and tales of excellent star-sightings that fulfilled the need their visitors so obviously had. Mission accomplished, after the string of jaw-dropping *no!*s and *really?*s and *shut-up!*s the guests uttered when informed that Kate Hudson often walked the beach with her son, Matthew McConaughey played Frisbee with his dog, Kiefer Sutherland went all Al-Gore-environment-guy about Malibu, Will Smith had a mansion just a few miles away, and John Mayer was reportedly checking out the spread next door.

Desi and Dash made the biggest impression by far,

however, when they told Crystal and Todd that party central, i.e., the Polaroid Beach House, famous for bashes and shenanigans involving all the young stars, was *within walking distance*, that Jacey had hosted the *Galaxy Rangers* wrap party there, and that in the wee hours of the morning you could sometimes hear music blasting, signaling some star-studded soiree in progress.

"Can we go there?" Todd asked, his copper eyelashes flashing with excitement. Todd didn't care that it was too early for any parties; he wanted to report home that he'd set foot on the same hallowed ground as . . . Lindsay! . . . and Britney! . . . and Cameron! . . . and, if his wish came true, and he won on *Gen Next*, it wouldn't be for the last time.

Garrett remained unfazed by the razzle-dazzle, but he was a good sport, listening and taking it all in. He asked if he could hang back while the others went for a swim.

Crystal was all about showing off her newly purchased, barely-there white bikini. Todd thought he might see stars 'boarding, catching a wave. Both were not-so-secretly hoping to be caught by paparazzi.

They'd have a better shot at being camera bait if Jacey hit the beach with them, so she slipped into her Miu Miu suit to indulge them.

"Indulge" was an understatement. The two crazy-glued

themselves to Jacey, who gave silent thanks for the fact that Ivy had slipped into a maillot and flip-flops and come along. The starstruck finalists turned out to be real motor-mouths when Garrett wasn't around.

Crystal's biggest fear was that she'd lose out to one of the guys, because the previous year's winner had been female. What did Jacey think?

What Jacey thought: wipe off the makeup; dial down the bling; and focus on your craft instead of the spoils of success.

What she said: "It's up to the voters, and on that count, I think you've got a great chance."

What *she* counted on: Crystal's conceits preventing her from reading between the lines of those carefully chosen words.

Todd, in his Nautica trunks ("I picked them out," Ivy bragged) displayed a more buff bod than Jacey had imagined. The boy *was* appealing, until he opened his mouth.

That was when he reminded her of Adam Pratt, who was basically okay but deeply superficial. "Is it true that you get paid just to show up at clubs?" Todd asked.

Crystal jumped in. "If you go to a club and sign autographs, you get paid. I read that LC from *The Hills* got enough to buy a pair of Marc Jacobs boots."

"Um, don't believe everything you read, okay?" Ivy said.

"When you go to clubs," Todd pressed, "they don't card you 'cause you're a star, right?"

Ivy took that one, too. "Clubs aren't such a big a deal. They're fun, but it's not like it looks in the magazines; not everyone goes every night. And even though they might not always card celebrities, Jacey doesn't drink in public. It wouldn't look good, especially to the *Generation Next* fans, you know?"

That stopped Todd momentarily, but not Crystal, already off in another equally chowder-headed direction. "How often do you get collagen injections for those lips?"

Jacey couldn't even *form* an answer. Were either of them going to ask a substantive question, or at least ask for a tip on winning?

Ivy assured Crystal that Jacey was all natural. Todd remained in fantasyland. "What about hook-ups? They're probably really easy if you're a star, right?"

Jacey's head began to spin. Crystal then peppered her with questions on stylists, and makeup artists, and which salon was best, and could she show Jacey her autograph book?—that is, the different ways she was trying out signing her name.

For the first time during her life in the spotlight, Jacey was actually thrilled when a pair of paparazzi descended upon them. It seemed the only way to shut Todd and

Crystal up. After posing with the finalists, Jacey suggested that the lensmen get some shots of the duo by themselves. "In a couple of weeks, I'll be yesterday's news—one of these two could easily be the next winner."

Jacey didn't really believe it, though. She was fairly sure Garrett would win, and after Crystal "accidentally on purpose" dropped a bikini strap, giving the photographers a nipple-peek, she prayed, *Please, America, do not send this misguided child to Hollywood.*

The impromptu 'razzi session was a big success. The cameramen walked away with an exclusive; Crystal and Todd felt like real stars. When Ivy suggested they all head back to the beach house for a dip in the Jacuzzi, Jacey was relieved. It meant the day was almost over. Or at least, her part of it was. Desi, Dash, and Ivy had already agreed to take the trio to dinner and a club. Without her.

The pulsing jets of the party-size circular hot tub were very relaxing. Jacey hadn't realized how tense she'd been all day. She leaned back against the smooth marble of the Jacuzzi and watched Crystal showing off her toe rings to Desi, who feigned interest; Dash turning down Todd's third request for a shot of tequila; and Garrett, sitting cross-legged by the side of the tub and smiling as Ivy laughingly reminisced about Jacey's playing Dora the Explorer in her third-grade play. "You should have seen it!

She cut her own hair, tried to dye it dark brown—what a disaster! Eight years old and already a method actress . . ."

"Why do you guys want to win?" Jacey asked, suddenly interrupting the general conversation.

Jacey guessed what their answers would be, but she hoped to be proved wrong.

She wasn't.

Crystal immediately shot her a What, Are You *New*? look, then exclaimed, "I want to be a star!"

"I want to be star, too!" Todd echoed. "And hook up with Lindsay Lohan!"

"Just to get the chance to act professionally? Is that enough reason to want to win?" Garrett's gaze went from Dash to Ivy to Jacey.

"Wait," Crystal said, her eyes narrowing. "Is this, like, a test or something?"

"Not at all," Jacey rushed to reassure her. "There are no wrong answers. I just wanted you to think about it."

"Look at Jacey," Garrett addressed his rivals. "She loves to act. And she's got this . . . house, this lifestyle, these great friends. She's found a way to have it all; maybe one of us, whoever wins, will, too."

Jacey nearly launched herself out of the hot tub to hug the boy. Crystal, predictably, stopped her in her tracks. "Oh! That reminds me, Jacey. I almost forgot to ask, who does your blog? How much would it cost to have them do mine?"

It was after two in the morning when Desi, Dash, and Ivy dragged themselves home from chaperoning and entertaining the "kids." Or, as Dash groused, reporting back to a still awake Jacey, "finishing up the job *you* agreed to!"

To which Jacey stubbornly retorted, "The job Ivy signed me up for!"

Whatever. Jacey was beyond grateful to her friends. By late afternoon, they had decided that no way, no how, could their starlet spend one more second with these misguided morons. Okay, two morons and one worthy contestant.

Graciously, intelligently, without bruising any egos or making any public gaffes that could backfire on Jacey, they had just dealt. They chauffeured Crystal, Todd, and Garrett to an excellent meal at Dolce, their favorite Italian restaurant, which happened to be co-owned by Ashton Kutcher. From there, they trooped to the nightclub Area and were rewarded with sightings of such night owls as Jessica and Ashlee. Drew Barrymore even stopped by their table to wish them all luck. As serendipity would finally have it, just before they left, Hayden Panettiere, the young actress who played the cheerleader on *Heroes*, showed up. Todd was in heaven.

"You get a raise—all of you," Jacey had declared when they came home.

"Good," Desi, aka, the Girl Who'd Gone from Payless to Prada in Record Time, said. "'Cause Chloe just came out with these boots I want."

"And I," Ivy said pointedly, "had to put up with paparazzi. They were so bummed that you weren't there, they had to resort to me! Can you believe they threw some crap at me about Emilio—my Emilio!—being seen with this other chick the past few nights? And those pushy jerks wanted to know how I felt about it!"

Ivy shook her head at what she assumed was a ridiculous question. She didn't seem to notice that Jacey tensed up, Desi turned away, and Dash changed the subject. "Why are you even up this late, anyway?" he asked Jacey. "Did you go out with Matt?"

Jacey had not. They'd talked and texted, but Jacey had pleaded fatigue when he'd asked to come over. She really was tired, but it was more that she was worried she'd slip up and let on how jealous she was. That would have done their budding relationship no good.

A question popped into her head now, though. It was for her friends. "When I was a contestant on *Generation*

*Next*, going through the auditions, week after week, none of you once asked me why I wanted to win so badly. How come?"

"We didn't need to," replied Ivy. "There was never any doubt. You were born to act."

"You got into this," Dash added, "not because you couldn't become anything else, but because you couldn't *not* become an actress."

Desi finished up with a shrug, "Your winning *Generation Next* just got you—and us—here sooner, is all. Good night, starlets."

# Chapter Ten

## And the Losers Are . . .

Crystal, Todd, or Garrett. Who would be eliminated tonight?

Judge Jacey could not have been more nervous if she'd been one of the contestants. She had all the symptoms—sweating, heart palpitations, and jitters—hoping that she—that is, Garrett—would make it to the finals. It depended on the voting public. They'd gotten it right last year. Jacey hoped they'd get it right again.

She couldn't let her feelings show. Not after her embarrassing blurt-out. If anything, she had to be more solicitous of the others, and as honestly critical of Garrett as possible. Tonight's show was live. Any inappropriate thing Jacey said would be held against her—and Garrett.

The show was a special one-hour version. For the first

half, the finalists would perform. Then, to allow America enough time to vote, the pop rockers The Orion Experience would perform for twenty minutes. Following that, the results would be announced, and the loser sent packing.

"Now, let's meet our judges!" Sean Brean, the show's host, said, looking into the camera. While he introduced Alex, Lloyd, and Miss Sabrina, Jacey took a moment to scan the audience: wow! It was jam-packed, and completely, wildly, out of control. *Gen Next* was not yet an *American Idol*-size hit, but its popularity would certainly rival it one day. ("Thanks to all the publicity you get," Ivy had sniffed. "They should give you kickbacks.")

Everyone in Hollywood wanted to be part of the live audience for the last two rounds. Producers, directors, judges, the camera crew, everyone connected with the show reported being barraged with ticket requests. A-listers like Reese Witherspoon had brought her kids, Tyra Banks and some of her top models were in the house, and so were J.Lo, Jessica, and Todd's crush, the *Heroes* cheerleader. Jacey's own posse, Ivy, Des, and Dash, had given up their seats for the biggest rock stars in the world: President Clinton, Senator Hillary Clinton, and Chelsea! How amazing was that?

She chuckled inwardly. Who wasn't there? Only Matt

Canseco and his too-cool-for-school crew. But Jacey knew Matt's little secret: he was watching it on TV that very moment!

The wildest, loudest noise-makers in the audience were the cheerleading squads for the contestants. The Hot Rod Todd contingent was revving their engines and waving posters for the redheaded finalist. Those in Crystal's Club displayed loyalty with—what else?— Swarovski crystals in their hair and glitter glued to their signs, posters, and banners. Jacey was scoping out Garrett's group when she thought she spied a familiar-looking pair in the audience. The only reason she noticed was because they *weren't* cheering for anyone; they were busy canoodling! Before she could focus on them, Sean started on her introduction. Jacey instantly turned toward the camera, grinned widely, waved, and winked—that last gesture was for her family, and for Matt.

Going live wasn't the only difference between this round and the previous ones. Tonight, the finalists could choose to do their scenes solo or with their rivals. They would also get professional help from the wardrobe, hair, and makeup departments.

Todd was first up. He brought a blond, pigtailed Crystal with him—and a miniskirted and bewigged Garrett. Jacey was puzzled, until the three broke out into song: *"Come and knock on our door. . . ."*

They were doing a scene from the classic TV knee-slapper *Three's Company.* Crystal was a perfect Chrissy—big boobs, squeaky voice, and dumb-bunny 'tude. And who knew Garrett could cross-dress so believably? He did total justice to the Janet Wood character. Todd cast himself, of course, as Jack Tripper, the klutzy lead that had been played by the late John Ritter.

The scene was hilarious—but was that due to the professional writing, the costumes, or the acting? If Todd had really wanted to demonstrate his comic chops, casting himself as one of the girls would've been a gutsier move.

Still, Todd had the audience on their feet and the judges well amused. Alex was howling; even the droll Lloyd let a giggle escape. Miss Sabrina was befuddled. "Toad, dear," she said, "was that *Some Like It Hot* you were doing? Were you supposed to be Tony Curtis? It pains me to say you weren't perfect. You missed his mannerisms entirely."

That was Todd's only negative review—the other judges were tickled. Jacey, trying to be extra nice, said, "You were fantastic, all of you. Wonderful choice, Todd. Once again, you really showed us your physical-comedy skill."

Then it was Crystal's turn. She chose to do her first act

with Garrett. What a surprise, thought Jacey. Crystal also went with a classic, the movie *Gone with the Wind*. Jacey's insta-take: she was relying far too much on the costumes. Her Scarlett O'Hara was in antebellum hoop-skirt overload.

What Crystal hadn't realized was that the most famous line in the scene wasn't Scarlett's. Garrett's Rhett Butler nailed lust-fueled frustration with the single sentence "Frankly, my dear, I don't give a damn." Frankly? It was as hot as anything Clark Gable had delivered, in Jacey's opinion.

Big misstep on Crystal's part. Jacey was sure one of the judges would point it out. To be safe, Jacey passed a note to Alex: *You say it—they already think I'm biased toward Garrett.*

*Because you want to jump his bones?* Alex wrote back. *Get in line!*

*Just say it!*

Alex did as requested, pointing out that while Crystal made a dramatic Scarlett, personally, he was all about Rhett. Lloyd felt Crystal had missed the mark by overdoing the histrionics. Miss Sabrina thought she'd underplayed it. Jacey, playing nicey-nice, gave Crystal "just right" kudos, explaining that the character was supposed to be self-absorbed and overdramatic.

Then it was Garrett's turn. Jacey's stomach lurched. *Please pick something good*, she prayed inwardly, while her face remained impassive. She needn't have worried.

Garrett did Shakespeare. By choosing the bitter soliloquy from the comedy *As You Like It*, Garrett evoked both poignancy and chuckles with his solo.

*All the world's a stage, and all the men and women merely players, they have their exits and their entrances. . . .*

When he got to the line *the lover, sighing like a furnace, with a woeful ballad,* Jacey would have bet he was looking straight at her.

All the judges, Jacey included, gave him major props. Miss Sabrina was so delighted her pinched face almost relaxed. "What justice you did to melancholy Jaques. Mr. Shakespeare would have been pleased, my dear."

Jacey checked the audience again at the two-minute commercial break, wondering if the lovers still needed to get a room. It wound up being Jacey who needed a room—a bathroom, to hurl in—when she figured out why they had looked familiar and confirmed they were still going at it.

Emilio and DeeDee? Jacey lunged out of her chair

with such force that she knocked it over. She hesitated for a half-second, deciding between stomping into the audience and racing backstage to ascertain what, if anything, Ivy had seen.

She had time for neither.

Alex promptly pulled her back down. "Five seconds," he said. "Hold it in."

"I don't have to pee," she said through gritted teeth. "I have to kill someone."

"Later," he said as the cameras blinked, and they were back, live.

Jacey's stomach churned up a storm through the entire second half of the show.

When the camera wasn't on her, she texted Matt: *Emilio's here! With her! You could have warned me!*

*I didn't know! She must have forced him to go with her*, Matt texted back.

*Did she force him to jump her bones right in the middle of a live show?*

*Everyone's watching the stage; no one's looking at them.*

*I am! And if Ivy is, the eruption will be epic.*

"Judge Jacey, it's your turn," Sean was saying. "What's your take on Todd's depiction of Raymond Babbitt in *Rain Man?*"

Judge Jacey hadn't been paying attention. But she was familiar with the Tom Cruise–and–Dustin Hoffman movie and went with her gut, which prompted her to say, "It rocked, Todd! I just wonder if you didn't play it too safe doing Raymond, the savant character. People might mistake that for a Dustin Hoffman impersonation. Tom Cruise's Charlie Babbitt is the tougher character."

She'd neither dissed nor overpraised it.

Because she hadn't been listening, though, she inadvertently said exactly what Lloyd had, only seconds before. *That* couldn't be good.

Jacey had to pay extra attention to Crystal and Garrett now—but how could she? She sneaked furtive glances at the audience at every opportunity, while craning her neck to see if Ivy was peeking from the wings.

Alex immediately saw what had caught Jacey's attention. He passed her a note that said, *Humpty-bumpty alert in aisle three! You know them?*

Jacey shot Alex a murderous look and tried to focus on Crystal, who did a complete one-eighty for this performance. She appeared onstage devoid of any makeup, wearing tattered rags. It was meant to be an homage to Charlize Theron, who had won an Oscar for the movie *Monster*, in which she played a serial killer. Crystal's interpretation, however, was not Oscarworthy. She must have thought that scrubbing off her makeup was enough to show the rawness and desperation of the character. It wasn't.

Meanwhile, Emilio and DeeDee continued their humpty-bumpty, coming up only for air. Jacey gave Crystal a much better review than the girl deserved, simply because she was distracted and panicked.

Why wouldn't they leave? Jacey willed it, but try as she would to communicate telepathically and teleport them out, her super powers would not kick in. Emilio and DeeDee stayed put.

The reason became ultra-apparent when Garrett went onstage: DeeDee was a huge fan. The blond boy had chosen a scene from the Christopher Reeve movie *Superman*. He didn't take the easy route; instead he played the lead as farm boy Clark Kent, devastated by the sudden death of his adoptive father, Jonathan. *"What good are all these powers,"* he cried out, *"if I couldn't even save my own father?"*

The judges were blown away. Even Miss Sabrina praised Garrett's introspective choice and moving performance. Tingles went up Jacey's spine. Her assessment had to be positive. It would be wrong to act otherwise just because people thought she favored him.

Jacey raced backstage at the break only to come upon

the most heartbreaking scene she'd ever witnessed. Ivy's heaving sobs were all too real. Dash and Desi were on either side of her, supporting her; even Garrett and Todd, who should have been sweating it out backstage, seemed upset and wanted to help.

"We're taking her home," Dash advised Jacey.

"Not without me," she said, summoning one of the assistant directors. "Please tell everyone I had an emergency and had to leave."

"You can't!" Desi hissed. "It's the elimination part."

"Exactly. It won't matter if I'm there or not."

Garrett jumped in. "She's not voting; she's really done with her job here."

Jacey didn't wait to get the okay from the producers. She led her devastated cousin out of the studio.

Ivy had seen the whole thing. At first, she'd been confused. Emilio hadn't mentioned the fact that he'd be in the *Generation Next* audience. If he'd told her he wanted to go, she'd have gotten him backstage with her.

Confusion turned to shock, and shock turned to intense, physical pain, rendering Ivy incapable of breathing. Hyperventilation had given way to pitiful, heaving sobs.

By the time they reached the beach house, Ivy's emotions had morphed once again. She was in a rage stage. Her fury was directed not at her cheating, double-dipping boyfriend; it was all for Jacey.

"How could you?" Ivy railed at her, her green eyes red and puffy, her cheeks stained strawberry.

"It's not Jacey's fault," Desi said gently.

"I'm sorry, Ives, I—we . . ." Jacey gulped, unsure what to say. She didn't know whether Ivy meant that Jacey had seen Emilio in the audience and not told her, or if she meant that Jacey had known all along.

"You knew—you all knew! And nobody told me! How could you?" Ivy wailed. "I thought you had my back. Turns out you're all better actors than anyone knew."

Ouch.

"I'm so sorry, I—" Jacey started.

"Don't. Lie. And don't make this about you, little starlet," Ivy sneered. "Think you can manage that? Just tell me the truth. How long has this been going on?"

"We're not sure—" Dash began, but Ivy wasn't having it. She stared daggers at Jacey. "How long?"

Jacey confessed they'd heard Emilio was cheating a month ago.

"But we didn't know it was with DeeDee!" Desi added, as if that made it okay.

"Oh, I believe that one," Ivy snapped. "'Cause Jacey

hates her, too! If this had had anything to do with the star of the household, we'd all have known about it. Obviously you found out at Matt's afterparty. That was the reason for your sudden ride on the vomit-comet, wasn't it? DeeDee was there, wasn't she? So, you got me away. Why didn't you tell me then? It was two weeks ago!"

"We hoped Emilio would man up," Jacey admitted.

"And when he didn't? When Matt couldn't convince him to, or didn't bother?—then what?"

"Don't, Ivy." Dash tried to reason with her. "We all thought—"

"Betraying me was a good idea? Is that what you were going to say, Dashiell?" Ivy was inconsolable. "You're all liars who don't care about anyone except yourselves and the meal ticket. You deceived me every bit as much as Emilio did."

Ivy stormed away and slammed the door to her room, leaving three guilt-ridden posse members distraught and miserable.

Ivy did not go to work the next day, or the day after that. It would take Desi, Dash, and Jacey several days of gentle cajoling and sincere apologizing, with lots of TLC, before the wounded Ivy emerged from her self-imposed hibernation.

Meanwhile, Jacey used the time to pressure Matt into

telling Emilio what happened: he'd been caught, and his girlfriend was flattened.

Matt still wouldn't get involved, but Jacey thought he might soften, for her sake.

Jacey's feeling was confirmed when Ivy told the group that Emilio had called her.

"What'd he say?" Jacey asked, handing Ivy a mug of soothing chamomile tea.

"Did he try to deny it?" Desi asked.

"He's not that stupid," Ivy said. "He gave me some garbage about me getting too 'business-y' for him. Whatever that means! Just because I have a job—it's only an internship—and I wear a suit sometimes, what's that got to do with anything?" Ivy started to tear up again.

"And he never said anything, just started cheating?" Jacey was indignant.

"Well, according to him, he did. He was all, 'I had to make an appointment to see you!'" Ivy huffed, imitating Emilio. "What? Did he expect me to live my life like he does—a complete slacker, mooching off the money machine?"

"If he really knew you, Ives, he'd have known all along that you're too smart, too talented not to have a career." Jacey said. Not only was that what Ivy needed to hear, it was the truth.

"You know the worst part?" Ivy sniffed. "He didn't even care if I saw him at the afterparty. Or at *Generation Next*! Was he thinking I'd be okay with this?"

"Maybe he was trying to make you jealous," Dash offered. "Which is kind of a compliment, in a juvenile way."

"Oh, please, all guys are jackasses. Even you, Dash. Even Matt," Ivy said.

"Matt?" Jacey repeated. "Why?"

"Is it so easy to forget that he cheated on you, too?" Ivy demanded.

Jacey felt as if she'd been kicked in the gut. "But . . . but . . ." she stammered, "Matt and I weren't together when that thing with Carlin happened."

"Puh-leez. He knew how you felt about him. Everyone did. He still hooked up with her, not one hundred yards from your house. Come on, Jacey."

Jacey flinched, stung by the memory. "That thing with Matt . . . You're right, it hurt like hell at the time. In the end, it was a speed bump in our relationship. Maybe this thing with Emilio . . . is, too?" she asked meekly, knowing full well how doubtful that was.

## jaceyfan blog

### Todd Gets Tossed; Jacey to Blame!

In a shocking turn of *Generation Next* events, Todd Forest got eliminated this week. Was it because of Jacey's blithe comment, which practically repeated word for word what Lloyd had just said? Two judges with the same opinion influenced the voters. What a shame!

Here's the real, secret shame. Jacey couldn't even be bothered to hang around for the voting results announcement. How rude! Get the boy tossed, then not even hang around to console him?

I have an even juicier bit of Judge Jacey news: the reason she dittoed another judge's comment? She wasn't paying attention—never saw Todd's performance, and never heard Lloyd's comment. Why? Her eyes were on the audience! Apparently, an interesting performance was going on there that distracted her from the one onstage.

In the real world, she'd be fired. Am I the only one who thinks she shouldn't be invited back for the final round? We all know who she's rooting for, anyway. *Generation Next* is on hiatus for the next three weeks because of the holidays. Which gives the producers plenty of time to think about it! Meanwhile, I'm asking you, the fans, to weigh in: does Jacey deserve to stay on as a judge, or should her sloppy attitude get *her* eliminated?

# Chapter Eleven

## Girls Go Wildin'

This is for Ivy, Jacey reminded herself, leading her cousin and Desi past the bouncer and through the velvet ropes that kept ordinary people out of Les Deux. Personally, she'd have been just as happy not to get into the Hollywood hot spot. Facing other stars and showbiz insiders meant putting on her starlet face, and after the last few drama-drenched days, she'd have preferred to stay in (with Matt, whom she hadn't seen much of since playing nursemaid to Ivy had cut the priority line).

Ivy had insisted on going to Les Deux tonight so she could scout new clients for Cinnamon.

Jacey wasn't buying it. What Ivy really wanted was to see if was Emilio was there—specifically, to see if he would dare to show up with DeeDee. Jacey dragged herself and Desi there to pick up the carnage.

At least Jacey liked this club. It wasn't only loud crowds, earsplitting music, and all standing–slash–dancing room. This club offered comfy sofas-only seating, upstairs and downstairs lounge areas, and an outdoor patio. DJs spun dance, Top 40, hip-hop, and rock.

To Jacey's dismay, Ivy made a beeline for the rock-walled patio, the hangout spot of choice for celebs, models, scions of rich families, and lushes—since bottle service ruled. Clearly, Ivy was counting on a painless evening, whether Emilio showed or not.

The threesome sat down on one of the supple black leather sofas that lined the patio. Ivy ordered a bottle of Grey Goose vodka and announced that it wasn't for sharing. Desi went ahead and asked for a pitcher of beer; Jacey, mindful of her underage status, asked if she could have Red Bull, for which Desi needled her, "That's the drink of rehab starlets all over town; I bet tomorrow's blog accuses you of having a drinking problem."

Meanwhile, Ivy craned her neck, trying to see around the three-tiered flowing fountain in the center of the patio. Jacey followed her gaze. There was plenty of star-gazing to be had: they spotted sisters Hilton, Olsen, and Simpson. Desi pointed out *Entourage* star Kevin

Connolly, Kid Rock, and post-rehab Jesse Metcalf from *Desperate Housewives.*

When they didn't see Emilio or any of Matt's other friends, Jacey felt safe enough to relax. She leaned back and looked up. The scent of jasmine was in the air—one of her favorite L.A. aromas. She noticed the ornate iron-work of the club's second-floor balconies above them, the peach-tinted mirrors on the walls, and the candelabras throughout the club. She didn't realize their drinks had arrived until Ivy was pouring herself a hefty vodka. "Do you know why Emilio used to take me here?"

Drink in hand, Ivy motioned toward the rock walls that enclosed the patio. "See the ivy plants twirling down the walls? He said they reminded him of me, and this would be our special place." She downed her drink and poured another, practically in one motion.

Eyeing the leafy stems that nearly covered the walls, Jacey's heart went out to her cousin. *Oh, crap, that's why we're here?* Jacey had never known Ivy to be a masochist. This breakup was doing a major emo-number on her. Jacey now started to hope they'd be interrupted.

No one seemed to be headed over to them, so Desi attempted to change the subject. "See that guy over there?" She nodded toward a hottie with shoulder-length dark hair who was slouching by the fountain. "The one giving off the 'Do me, I'm sensitive' vibe? A few more glasses of beer, and I could."

"Desi!" Jacey squealed. "What about Mike—isn't he still in your life?"

"Mike's in Hawaii, at a surfing competition. He won't be back for weeks. Besides, he was fun while he lasted."

"And now you're past it?" Jacey said, looking meaningfully at Ivy, hoping to draw her into Desi's silly fantasy life.

Didn't work.

Ivy was in her own world, misty-eyed as she gestured toward the patio. "And he always said I looked the most beautiful under that lamp."

A giggle escaped Desi's glossed lips.

"What?" Ivy demanded.

Oh, great, Jacey thought. *Now* she's paying attention.

"Nothing." Desi seemed to change her mind.

"I said, *what*?" Ivy growled. "Something's funny about me and Emilio?"

Desi gulped, than gave it up. "When I told Dash we were coming here, he said this club had special lighting that could make a toad look good."

So that she wouldn't burst out laughing, Jacey went into her famous (well, in third grade, anyway) frog croak. She did a dead-on *Ribbit! Ribbit!* It had used to kill Ivy.

Now, however, instead of being amused, Ivy looked ready to kill Desi.

"Jacey! Omigod, I haven't seen you in, like, hours! Is *Gen Next* taking up all your time?"

Jacey had never been so happy to see Kate Summers in her entire life. Even if everything that came out of her mouth was inane and even if the equally bubble-brained Sierra Tucson was by her side.

"What's the inside word on *Gen Next*? Why didn't you stay for the elimination results? Did you already know Garrett was safe?" Sierra was off and babbling.

"Sorry to disappoint," Jacey said. "I don't have any inside word."

"She really did have to leave," Ivy told them. "Her big emergency was me."

Two pairs of professionally plucked and waxed eyebrows arched. "Do tell," urged the gossip-crazed Kate.

To be sure Ivy wouldn't, Desi improvised. "Ivy got a call that Jacey was needed at an audition, exactly at that moment."

Ooops, bad idea, Des, since the idea of any actress snaring an audition, or worse, a gig, that neither Kate nor Sierra knew about invited more questions.

"What was it for? Can you tell us?" they chorused.

"No, it wasn't a part for me," Jacey explained. "They're

starting auditions for *Supergirl*, and they needed me there, that's all."

"They're casting?" Sierra asked. "I thought they hadn't started."

"Best get your agent on it," Jacey advised. "Never too soon."

Jacey and Desi had a good laugh as the two starlets tried to beat each other to their BlackBerries. Even Ivy managed a half-smile.

The arrival of Kate and Sierra at their table marked the beginning of a steady stream of drive-by celebrity table-hopping. Luckily, it kept Ivy's mind off Emilio.

"Everyone except Matt, that is." Ivy was on her third or fourth drink, and Jacey, talking to Ashley Olsen, turned around to face her cousin, who'd been chatting Mary-Kate up.

"What were you saying, Ivy?" Jacey asked suspiciously.

"Oh, I was just telling M.K. that I didn't think Matt would have come to the *Galaxy Rangers* premiere even if he had been available. He doesn't believe in that kind of thing."

A red flag went up in Jacey's head. Intuition told her that Ivy was getting on an express train that wouldn't stop until she said something they'd all regret. Jacey purposely hadn't touched any liquor, just so she could react reasonably if Ivy got in her face.

Jacey turned back to her own conversation until Ivy's next insult: "Too bad Matt's not into Jacey enough to overcome his snotty attitude about premieres and awards shows. You'd think he'd make an exception for her."

Desi swooped in to the rescue. "Let's dance," the little one shouted. "I love this song!" Mighty-mite Desi grabbed the way taller Ivy and yanked her off the sofa and on to the dance floor. Jacey followed. In minutes, they'd joined the dancing crowd, singing and swiveling their hips to "Don't Cha?"

"Let's keep her dancing," Jacey whispered to Des.

Desi gave Jacey a thumbs-up. After a few more gyrating grooves, however, Ivy managed to pour herself another drink. The booze did not obliterate her obsession. It didn't matter if the girls were on the dance floor, karaoke-ing, or partying with others; Ivy was on a streak.

"You and Matt are just like me and Emilio," Ivy slurred.

Jacey suppressed a scowl. "How's that?"

"Once he's over the sex, he'll realize who you really are—"

"Meaning?" Jacey knew she shouldn't be letting Ivy goad her. But the crack about Matt's not caring still stung.

"You're America's sweetheart. You're everything he truly despises—"

Desi danced over and inserted herself between them while warbling, *"To the left, to the left . . ."* from Beyoncé's "Irreplaceable."

Jacey didn't take the cue. She still felt guilty about betraying Ivy. She wished she could rewind the past couple of weeks and do things differently, but Ivy's putting Jacey, Matt, and the word *despises* in the same sentence was just wrong. There would be consequences.

"You're famous, you're rich, you're glitzed-up for red-carpet events, you're Hollywood girl." Ivy's finger was dangerously close to Jacey's face. "Matt hates all that stuff. Do not deny it!"

Desi wrapped her arm around Jacey's waist and whirled her a few feet away from Ivy the Awful. "Let it go," Desi was saying. "She's not in her right mind."

*Does that mean everything she's hurling at me is wrong?* Jacey couldn't stop that thought from popping up.

Ivy *still* would not let it go. "Why do you think Matt the Movie Star never had run-ins with the media before you?"

Jacey took a deep breath and turned away.

Ivy grabbed her bicep and forcibly turned her around. "He trashes bars, smashes hotel rooms, hates the paparazzi, but he's never raged on them. Wanna know why?"

Jacey could feel her face reddening. "Enlighten me."

"Because Matt avoids them, that's why. He goes to dive bars and dates Goth girl nobodies. It's only when he's with you that paparazzi follow. And just how long do you think he's gonna stand for that?" Ivy's smirk was evil. Jacey's eyes narrowed.

Desi, bless her little heart, would not stop intervening. Not aware of the fresh can of venom Ivy was about to pop open, Des dragged Kate and Sierra over with her—inadvertently giving them grist for more gossip.

"You're the symbol of everything he hates. You're candy-girl Sandy; he's James Dean. You're the anti-Matt. You always were. Face it, little Miss Virgin. There's no future in this relationship."

Jacey's eyes started to puddle, and it got harder and harder to remind herself that Ivy had every right to vent; she'd been dumped, cheated on, and kept in the dark by her best friends. Jacey knew she should just suck it up. She deserved it. What she didn't deserve was the entire club's hearing it. And there was this: if she didn't buy a word of Ivy's rant, then why was she choking down that knot in her throat?

Desi got the DJ to turn the music up to try to drown Ivy out.

Didn't work.

If anyone had missed Ivy's acting out before, this time the whole patio at Les Deux got an earful of Ivy pointing to the heavens and thundering, "Supergirl! Look, up in the sky! It's a bird, it's a plane—it's the slut Matt slept with!"

Famous jaws fell open all over the room. All eyes were trained on the balcony. There, a horrified duo peered down at the spectacle Ivy was making of herself.

Kia the Creepy was one half of the duo; Carlin McClusky was the other. Carlin, the wannabe comic actress who'd lost to Jacey on *Generation Next*—Carlin, with her Barbie-doll figure and long, lustrous blond hair, who'd seduced Matt practically right outside the beach house door. Never seeing *her* again would have been too soon for Jacey.

Sensing she'd need it, someone placed a bottle in Jacey's hand. The grateful starlet took a gulp. It tasted like iron, burned her throat, and made her eyes water. Tequila. She took another swig.

"What the hell are they doing here?" Desi looked at Ivy as if she were responsible for setting the whole thing up to get back at Jacey. "I'm going up there and chasing them out."

"No, you're not," Ivy, now wobbling precariously,

slurred. "They have a right to be here. Kia's probably scouting for Cimm-na-min. And Carlin, ha! She's a ho. Probably on the lookout for her next victim."

Sierra, of all people, remained cool. She seemed to recall that Jacey had once bailed Kate and her out of an embarrassing, booze-fueled situation. That was probably why she tapped Desi on the shoulder and said, "You guys should sit down and eat something."

She meant well enough, but she didn't know that Les Deux didn't serve food.

"Desserts only," Kate put in.

The promise of sweets distracted Desi momentarily. "Really? Just desserts?"

"Cupcakes—" Kate started to recite the different kinds, but Ivy picked up the thread, thrust her refilled glass in the air and hollered, "To just desserts! Woo-hoo— I hope all the jerks get their . . ."—she belched loudly—"just desserts tonight!"

Before anyone could make a move, Kia and Carlin were down onto the patio getting into Ivy's face. "What did you call me?" Carlin screeched at Ivy, tossing her sticky, Jack-infused soda at her.

Drenched and drunk, Ivy raised her arm threateningly, ready to smash her glass over Carlin's head. Kia, who'd doused Desi with her rum and Coke, rushed between them and pushed Ivy backward into the three-tiered concrete fountain instead. Ivy's glass flew backward in the air, bulls-eyeing an expensive bottle of champagne on a waiter's tray.

Jacey ran over to pull Ivy out of the gurgling water, only to have Carlin come up behind her and shove her in, too. As she did a face-plant into the fountain, Jacey's legs flew up in the air, and she instantly regretted having worn a tight mini. If someone had sneaked a camera into the place, the entire world would have gotten a close-up of what she'd bought on her last visit to Victoria's Secret.

Jacey was furious, Ivy more so.

Ivy had managed to right herself, but wasn't sober enough to get out of the fountain. A cute guy extended his arm, but she grabbed his drink instead and threw it at Carlin. Then Desi kicked Carlin in the butt. She had just whirled around to slug Kia when two beefy security men snatched her. Desi disliked being manhandled and tried her best to break free. Jacey and Ivy climbed out of the fountain and were going over to help when club reinforcements arrived.

Kicking and screaming, the starlet and her posse pals were unceremoniously tossed out of Les Deux on their cute "les tushes." The management was gracious enough to send them away with cupcakes, and towels to dry off with.

"Nice work, Dimples. I like your style," Matt teased. "Wish I'd been there to see it."

It was well past three in the morning, but Jacey hadn't wanted to go home. She put Ivy and Desi in a limo, then phoned Matt to come and get her. Now he was gently ragging on her. "You only call me when you need advice or rescuing, huh?"

Jacey needed reassurance. She needed to know that nothing Ivy had spewed at her was even remotely true, that Matt wasn't going to kick her to the curb because she represented everything about showbiz he "despised."

"Where to?" he asked, glancing over at her from the driver's seat. "Wait, I should get you home to change into dry clothes first."

"Not home," she said, realizing she was in danger of slurring her words. "I need to talk to you."

He stopped at a light and seemed to consider. "Okay, Dimples. Hang on a second." Matt turned onto a darkened side street. He drove for a while to get away from the main drag. Then he pulled over and turned the engine off.

"Why are we here?" Jacey asked.

"You'll see in a minute." He pulled his long-sleeved shirt off over his head and handed it to her. "Scooch down on the floor and take all your wet stuff off, dry yourself with the towel, and put this on. It should be long enough to cover you—maybe even longer than that micromini you have on. Which smells like booze, by the way."

Jacey inhaled sharply, staring at his smooth, toned chest and sinewy arms. In the soft glow of the streetlight, he looked amazing.

"Stop staring. Go ahead, change, I'll shield you from drive-bys."

Jacey did as he told her and was immediately glad she had. She felt instantly better once out of her sticky, smelly clothes. Being completely naked in Matt's soft T-shirt, inches from him in the jump seat of his sports car, was pretty sexy, too.

Then Ivy's hurtful words came back to her. She stared straight out at the street. "Am I too much trouble for you, Matt?"

"What? Because you call me at two in the morning to come get you? You're my girl. It's no trouble—whenever I can be with you it's all pleasure."

Jacey tried again. "You hate stuff like red carpets, and big movies, and paparazzi."

"That's true," he said carefully. "I'm not into that scene." She sensed that he was staring at her, but she couldn't bring herself to face him. Not yet.

"I'm symbolic." She choked back unexpected tears, so it came out *sym-boc-tic.*

"You're drunk," Matt said kindly. "That's all."

The sweetness in his voice, the caring and understanding, was what did it. Everything came spilling out of her. In spite of herself, she had taken Ivy's words to heart. Now, she recited them to Matt, sobbing like a child.

Matt pressed her against his bare chest. He wrapped his arms around her and sang, *"Show a little faith, there's magic in the night."*

"Huh?"

"Springsteen."

She sniffled and gazed up at him through damp eyelashes. "I don't understand."

"It just means sometimes you have to take a leap of faith. We have some big differences, but we're not blind; we know what they are. And I guess in some ways, like you with the paparazzi in your face, I'm gonna have to do some adjusting. I get that. You're gonna have to do some, too, Dimples."

She knew then and there that Ivy had been right. He wouldn't have gone to the *Galaxy Rangers* premiere, no matter how much she'd wanted him to.

"I know who *I* am, Jacey."

"So what are you saying? That I don't know who I am? Or what I believe in?" she asked.

"I'm saying," he said, as he kissed the top of her head, "that I've had four more years to figure it out. Eight more in Hollywood, in this business. You're still going through so many firsts: first good reviews; first lousy ones; first unfair rejection; first . . ." he trailed off.

". . . First time I betrayed my cousin?" She filled it in.

"A lot of firsts, that's all. You'll figure out what's right."

*Will you wait for me to catch up?* That was what Jacey wanted to say. But she remained silent.

"Ivy was wrong, Dimples. You're not a symbol to me. You're Jacey, the girl I'm crazy about. And soon, a real woman. I'm not going anywhere."

They kissed softly at first. There wasn't much room to maneuver in his tiny two-seater, but Matt slid the seat back as far as it would go, and Jacey hoisted herself onto his lap. She kissed his cheeks, his neck, his shoulders. She ran her hands through his thick, wavy hair. Their kisses were getting more intense, and Matt's hands were on her thighs, caressing her, heading northward.

She wanted to . . . she wanted to. But . . . what if Ivy

was right? What if it was over after they had sex? If she didn't put the brakes on right now, she wasn't sure she'd be able to at all. Jacey couldn't bear the thought of what might happen then.

## Club Crawl Leads to Bully Brawl!

Oh, what a night! If only you, the people who voted for Jacey, to whom she owes her career and her enviable new life, could've been there. You would have seen Jacey's true Oscar-worthy performance—she was way more believable playing a drunken diva than a sober space heroine. Lucky for you, you've got me, and I was there. Here's an eyewitness account of Jacey's latest embarrassment to us all.

Let's start with why an underage starlet was even in a hot nightclub in the first place—then, let's ask why she was quaffing tequila straight from the bottle. I must have missed it when they changed the law to legalize liquor for seventeen-year-olds.

The fearsome threesome, Jacey, Ivy, and Desi, arrived at Les Deux's celebrity-loaded patio area, where bottle service began before their bottoms even hit the sofas. Well lubricated, they proceeded to mock Kate Summers and Sierra Tucson by making them believe casting for *Supergirl* had started. I happen to know that the auditions won't begin until January.

After trading giggles and one-ups with other table-grazing celebs, the trio hit the dance floor, completely toasted. That's when the truly rude, lewd, and crude behavior began.

Poison Ivy started it by calling comic actress Carlin McClusky, who was innocently minding her own business, an unprintable name.

Desi-Destructo proceeded to punch out Carlin's innocent friend Kia. The tiny terror followed up by flinging her drink in Carlin's face.

Juiced Jacey helped shove the victimized Carlin into a fountain—and that's what started the full-out brawl. Fists flew, bottles broke, another round of drinks went flying. A dunking in the fountain wasn't enough to cool Jacey off—the drenched starlet kicked and screamed as her posse of bullies finally got ejected from the club. And who did Jacey call to dry her off? Who do you think? The master club-trasher himself, Matt Canseco.

I said it before, and I'm sticking by it: hooking up with bad boy Matt Canseco will lead Jacey only to disaster. After tonight, I rest my case.

# Chapter Twelve

## Meeting Cute

"Have you lost your posse, little girl?"

Jacey smiled at the sound of the familiar voice and whipped around. "Garrett, hi!"

"What are you doing here?" They said it at the same time—then laughed.

"Christmas shopping." Again, same words, same time.

They'd bumped into each other at the Farmers Market, L.A.'s colorful open-air market that displayed everything from fresh edibles to oddball collectibles. It was in the late morning, a few days before Christmas, and the place was packed with last-minute shoppers.

"Are you really here alone? No bodyguards, no posse?" Garrett asked, looking around.

"Starlet escapes!" Jacey giggled. "That'll be the head-line of tomorrow's blog. Unless you give me up."

"Your secret's safe with me," he promised. "But seriously, what if you get recognized? You could be mobbed."

Jacey pointed to her baseball cap and dark shades and affected a deep voice. "This is the universally recognized celebrity-going-incognito look—totally effective, until you came along."

Garrett laughed. "Hey, I saw a cute girl, stopped, and then recognized your hair. I was pretty sure it was you, but . . . Jacey Chandliss, in the Farmers Market? Does not compute."

"Too downscale for a star of my caliber? Is that what you mean?" Jacey teased him.

Garrett blushed slightly. "Well, it's not exactly Melrose Avenue."

"Precisely why I'm here," Jacey replied. "I'm on a reconnaissance mission, searching for a special gift for someone who's anti-extravagance."

"That someone being Matt Canseco?" Garrett guessed.

Jacey's eyes widened. Had she been that transparent?

"Sorry," Garrett said quickly. "None of my business."

Jacey noticed his large shopping bag. "Who're you shopping for?"

"Everyone on my list," Garrett said. "This is one of the few places in L.A. where I can afford to shop, and, since I leave for home tomorrow, I have to get it all done."

"Remind me where home is?"

"Small town called Narrowsburg," Garrett replied.

"Oh, that's right," Jacey said, remembering. Then, impulsively, she asked, "Are you hungry, by any chance?"

"Always," he said, patting his concave stomach. "I'm a growing boy."

"I've been so tempted to nosh," she admitted. "All this yummy food." She nodded toward stalls packed with juicy-looking fruit, shellfish on ice, inviting displays of cheeses and dips, freshly baked bread, and pastries.

"I think I've got enough left in my wallet for a treat," Garrett said. "What are you in the mood for?"

"Everything!" Jacey said. "How about we grab a basket, fill it with whatever looks tempting, and do a picnic?"

"That," Garrett said, "is a great idea."

"Only I'm paying for everything. Otherwise, it'd be just my luck that we both get recognized and you wind up looking like you tried to bribe a judge."

"You don't have a vote," Garrett pointed out. "Why would I bribe you?"

"Ah, but my pithy comments can influence voters. I've

already messed up enough on that count, as you well know."

A blush crept up Garrett's neck. "It's down to me and Crystal, and I think most voters have already decided. Anyway, I think we're cool as long as we don't talk about the scenes I'm going to do and you don't give me any advice."

Jacey wasn't completely convinced. "Hang on. I don't want to get you in trouble." She called Dash and asked him to check with *Gen Next*'s producers to be sure they weren't breaking any rules.

In the meantime, Jacey and Garrett cruised the stalls and stands, picking up bread, cold cuts, cheeses, baby carrots, dips, cherries, bunches of grapes, and even a couple of cooked lobster claws.

Dash called back. There was nothing in the *Gen Next* rules preventing them from having lunch—but anything more than that might look suspicious to the voters.

"That's only if anyone sees us," Jacey reminded him.

"Stop being naive," Dash said. "You're in a public place. Just eat fast, no touching, and send the boy on his way."

It wasn't as if Jacey *planned* to disregard Dash's advice. It just happened that way.

Garrett found them a picnic table on the fringes of the

market, as far from the crowds as possible. For extra insurance, he tilted its sunshade umbrella to shield them from inquiring eyes, especially those attached to camera lenses.

Garrett made a turkey sandwich and gave half to Jacey.

"Are you excited to be going home?" she asked, munching away.

"Sort of," he answered honestly. "I'd rather go home after I won. Or lost."

Jacey avoided eye contact, slicing a wedge of cheese with a plastic knife.

"Winning a competition like *Generation Next*," she said, "can be a blessing and a curse."

Garrett wrinkled his forehead and nodded solemnly. "Copy that! Being out here in Holly-weird, I see things very differently than I did before."

"See *and* read all about it," Jacey said, referring to the Les Deux debacle, still a hot topic on E!, *Extra*, and *ET*, as well as being headline news in the supermarket tabs.

"Everyone is talking about it," Garrett conceded.

"The amazing exploits of Jacey and her all-girl fighting posse!" she joked. Although it was obvious Garrett wanted to know more, Jacey decided against it for now. She quickly changed the subject. "Show me the gifts you bought. Maybe I'll find something to inspire me."

"Doubtful," Garrett said. "Cheapie souvenirs, mostly, but that's what the folks back home will like."

"I get that," Jacey told him. "I sent all kinds of souvenirs home during my first few weeks out here—they loved them!"

It happened while Garrett was displaying his purchases. He leaned over to hand each one to her. Their foreheads may have bumped, their hands brushed against each other—several times. Jacey gave it no thought; they were friends.

Garrett had bought a Los Angeles T-shirt for his brother, diaries and funky hats for his sisters, and a mug for his mom. He hadn't found anything for his dad yet.

"What does he like to do?" Jacey asked.

"He's a typical dad, I guess. Watches sports, plays basketball, mows the lawn, barbecues every Sunday. Loves to eat."

Jacey snapped her fingers. "I've got it! Come with me."

Linking her arm through his, Jacey navigated their way through the crowded market to a store called Light My Fire. "They sell all kinds of hot sauces, rated from mild to five-alarm fire."

Garrett's eyes lit up when he saw that Jacey wasn't

kidding. "Wow—this place rocks!" he exclaimed. His throat heated up once he started taste-testing the sauces. He dipped his finger into a sample from Red Hot Chili-Peppers and held it up for Jacey to lick. Neither noticed the customer who'd been following them, snapping cell-phone pictures.

"I have some other ideas," Jacey told him. "If you want to add a little more L.A. 'flava' to your booty."

Garrett was up for it.

His mom and sisters had to have sunglasses, Jacey told him. "Way more L.A. than T-shirts."

She took him to Duck Soup, the go-to stall for rocks, robots, and games that Garrett's brother might like. Sticker Planet was the place for stocking-stuffers for the girls.

As the afternoon wore on, the crowds got thicker. Jacey and Garrett had to stay close together or risk losing each other. To avoid being recognized, Jacey turned more than once and pressed her head into Garrett's chest. He shielded her with his arm. They were fairly sure no one had noticed them.

"What about your girlfriend? Need anything for her . . . ?" Jacey asked, totally fishing.

"I don't have one," Garrett replied.

"That's smart," Jacey heard herself say inanely. "Wait

until after the holidays for a girlfriend—it'll save you money."

He laughed. "Anyway, thanks so much for the help. I owe you." That was when it happened again. He was only trying to show her his appreciation. He put his arm around her and tried to kiss her cheek, but Jacey swiveled her head, and the kiss ended up on her lips. They pulled apart awkwardly.

"Um," Garrett said, "can I repay the favor and help you find something for Matt?"

"Maybe," Jacey agreed. "I've got nothing."

"What do you think he'd like? Clothes? CDs? DVDs? Books? Vintage movie poster? Video iPod? A mix tape?"

She burst out laughing, "A mix tape, that's so great! Maybe if we'd met in 1999!"

"You're not helping here," Garrett pointed out. "You wanted something unique, right? I'm trying to come up with something."

"I just want something different. Something that expresses—"

"—How you feel about him?" Garrett guessed.

"Kind of," she mumbled, pulling the brim of her cap lower to hide the blush she felt creeping over her face.

"Let me think. What would I want if I had an amazing girlfriend like you?"

Jacey wished he hadn't said that. Wished, too, that her tummy weren't doing a flip-flop.

"I'd want . . . I'd want . . . time alone with her," Garrett mused. "Okay, if it was her present to me, I'd want her to plan a special night. How's that?"

"Continue."

Garrett looked surprised. "Really? I'm improvising. Making this up."

"Let's see what you got." Jacey tried to sound as if she were ribbing him. "You started it."

"Okay," Garrett agreed. "I like to eat, so a home-cooked meal would—"

"—Not gonna happen." Jacey stopped him right there. "If I cook, odds are he doesn't live to tell about it."

Garrett laughed. "Scratch that. Go with a home-catered meal. But set the atmosphere: flowers on the table, dim lighting, candles. I'd hope some romantic music was on, and maybe we'd dance a little. Slowly."

"You are so having fun with this," Jacey said. "What else?"

"Well, I'd assume she'd be wearing something sexy the whole time. . . ." He trailed off and winked.

"And then?"

"You know what, Chandliss, I think the evening would proceed naturally after that."

"Not too shoddy, McKinley," Jacey acknowledged. "That might be a nice gift—for the right person, that is. I will take it under advisement. Now, where's your car parked?"

"I don't have a car. I took the bus."

Duh. She'd forgotten. "I hope you didn't buy a round trip. I'm taking you home."

Still, neither Jacey nor Garrett noticed the person following them, taking pictures.

Garrett asked about her holiday plans on the ride back. Jacey had decided to stay in Malibu until her mom had the baby, sometime in January. Then, she'd fly home.

"Will Desi, Dash, and Ivy stay, too?" he asked.

"They're going back to Michigan," she said. "They get some time off. I'm a benevolent dictator."

He chuckled. "Won't you be lonely over the holidays? Oh, wait, won't Matt be around to keep you company?"

"Matt lives here, so, yeah, he should be around."

"Speaking of Matt . . ." he paused. "Do you mind if I ask you a personal question?"

Jacey shot him a sidelong glance. What did he have in mind?

"Forget it, I'm being too nosy," Garrett said.

"No, it's all right, you can ask. Doesn't mean I have to answer."

"You and Matt, you guys are together, right? And your movies came out the same day. *Dirt Nap* was well received, but *Galaxy Rangers*, not so much. So I'm just wondering if that makes it hard on your relationship."

Jacey considered her answer. Lie? Be honest? Be vague?

"There were a lot of reasons I chose to do *Galaxy Rangers*," Jacey said truthfully. "I knew it was fluff when I signed on. Matt . . . well, Matt does his thing. He can. He doesn't have the same kind of PG-rated responsibility to an audience who voted for him—you catch my meaning?"

Garrett's face turned serious. "I guess I do. I guess I better!"

"So, yeah," Jacey continued, "I do feel a little jealous that he gets to experiment, to stretch his acting wings, while I—well, you get the point."

"But you're optimistic, right? You believe it won't get in the way of your relationship."

Garrett wasn't questioning it.

It was late afternoon by the time Jacey returned to the beach house. Already, the sun was starting to set—a reminder that even though southern California stayed warm year-round, darkness came well before evening in the winter months. That kind of planetary reality check was necessary, 'cause, aside from the cheesy, phony decorations around town, no way did it look like Christmas in Malibu. Not with the ocean so blue, the sparkling sand, the thong-birds (as Dash called the scantily clad girls) and their surfer dudes strolling along the beach.

Jacey didn't miss winter in Michigan; she didn't pine for the evergreens, the snow, the slippery ice-capades that came with driving in blizzard conditions. She missed her family, but not the biting winds. She was here now. So were her closest friends. What were the chances, she wondered idly, that she could convince her family to move out west? How excellent would that be if she did? She smiled just thinking about it. But her smile faded when she thought of something Garrett had said. He'd inadvertently touched on a sore spot about her and Matt. She was totally putting the "lousy" in "jealousy"—it was getting worse, not better.

And that, she said, scolding herself as she strode into the living room, was the kind of destructive thinking that needed to be banished if she and Matt were going to have a chance at keeping their relationship together.

She still had no gift for him.

"Greetings, my pensive princess of the market," Dash said, looking up from his laptop. "Why so glum? And why so . . . empty-handed? Should I signal the butler to haul in your purchases? Or will it take a bevy of butlers?"

Jacey plopped down on the sofa next to Dash and rested her head on his shoulder. He put his arm around her waist. "Hey, I was kidding," he said. "What's wrong?"

"Nothing," she lied.

"It's Garrett, isn't it?" Dash pulled away so he could look directly into her eyes. "I knew it! What happened? Did the paparazzi catch you? Did you get him disqualified, or worse?"

"No, no, and, nothing. Not in that order."

"For an award-nominated actress, you're not very convincing. C'mon, give it up. Uncle Dash is here for you."

Jacey curled up and helped herself to some of Dash's still-steaming latte.

"Of course you may share my java," he said teasing her. "Shall I also fetch you a scone?"

She smiled. How she loved Dash. "You alone? Where is everyone?"

Dash gave her a funny look. "Did you forget that Ivy left?"

Duh. That was right, her cousin had decided to go home early, hoping a few extra days with family would help fix what Emilio had broken. Jacey had sent Ivy's Christmas gift, a Louis Vuitton business tote with her initials embossed on it, to Michigan instead of giving it to her in person.

"And Desi is . . ." Dash stopped to think. "Not sure."

Jacey found it odd for Dash to be unaware of Desi's whereabouts. After she'd crashed Jacey's Mercedes, there'd been a moratorium on her driving alone. Even sober, the girl wasn't safe. "Did she take one of the cars?"

Dash fidgeted with his Livestrong wristband. "Maybe."

Okay, now he's lying. He knows where she is, Jacey thought. He's not saying because—oh, wait, Des could be Christmas-shopping for her.

"Fine, be that way." She pretended to brush him off.

"So, what's up with you, anyway?" Dash asked again, "Regretting bumping into Garrett?"

"We had fun. I helped him pick out a bunch of presents for his family," Jacey said, draining the latte.

"Then what?" Dash probed. "You're feeling sucky about something."

She sighed. Maybe it would feel better to talk it out. There was no one on earth safer to confide in than Dashiell Walker, her secret-keeper, her conscience, her soul mate. If only he'd been straight. Ah, they'd have been so perfect.

Scratch that. Dash was like her brother. Matt was the one who made her heart take flight. Jacey had never felt that way about any guy before. Not even her high school boyfriend, the basketball star–slash–valedictorian she'd once planned to marry—the guy she'd wanted to be her "first." Things didn't happen as planned. She got famous, she got dumped, and she got to Hollywood, still a virgin.

"There's something about Garrett," she told Dash now, "I'm just not sure what."

"Everyone knows you think he's hot," Dash said.

"Off point," she scowled.

"Enlighten me. What *is* the point?"

"In some ways, he's more in sync with me than Matt is." There, she'd said it.

"In what ways?" Dash pressed, his tone wary. "You mean, because he's coming from the same place you did, a potential out-of-nowhere winner?"

Maybe that was part of it, Jacey admitted to herself. Garrett was as wide-eyed and awestruck at Hollywood as she'd been once—and still was, in many ways—while remaining totally serious about acting. "He's smart. He can already see how much phoniness and backstabbing goes on here, but he still believes in—God, this is corny—the magic of Hollywood. Like I do. Kind of."

Dash folded his arms over his chest and frowned. "Is it possible Garrett is playing you? Think about it, Jace. This is a kid who's one competitor away from living a fantasy life—and doesn't he come from a farm or something?"

"So what are you saying?" Jacey's back was up.

"You've only just met this dude, and you're in a position to do something for him. You can't forget that. Maybe his real talent is figuring out what you want to hear, then echoing it back to you."

"And what do I want to hear?" she asked defensively.

"Oh, the usual," Dash said. "How awesome you are, how you're able to have it all—without giving up the street cred of being a serious actress. Isn't that what he said?"

"Kind of," she admitted grudgingly. "But so what?"

"So, Jacey . . . isn't that exactly how you'd like to see yourself?"

She stiffened. Dash was probing, in dangerous emotional territory, even for him. She pressed her lips together. "Not sure I like where you're going with this."

"It's very clear, love. The last round of *Generation Next* is in a few weeks, after the holidays. He gets *you*, last year's very successful winner, to gush over him on camera, which could push him over the finish line, ahead of Scarlett whatsherface."

"Crystal. Not Scarlett," Jacey mumbled. "But you're wrong, Dash. I can tell when someone's being real."

"Look, sweetie," Dash purred. "You know I'd do anything for you. 'Anything' includes telling you the truth, whether you want to hear it or not. Here's what I see: Matt Canseco has never, not once, lied to you, whether you agree with him or not, whether you want to hear it or not. He's been honest, unlike—do I have to point out—some of his friends? If you guys are together, that's a deep thing, Jacey. Why would you let Garrett influence you? Don't kick to the curb what you fought so hard to win. You've got Matt's heart. You can't expect him to give up his principles—in the end, you wouldn't respect him if he did. And you can't truly love someone you don't respect."

"When did I ask for the essay answer?" Jacey grumbled, hauling herself off the sofa. "I'm going upstairs to shower."

"Wait," Dash said. "We need to talk about something else."

"Ivy?" Jacey guessed.

"No, Shelter Rock. I've looked into it as thoroughly as I can. It seems to be on the level. No skeletons in the closet that I could find. It looks like money you donated, or raised, would go directly to those kids."

"So you think I should forget other charities and be the major benefactor for the place?" Jacey asked.

"I wouldn't be opposed," Dash said, training his eyes on the laptop screen. He turned it around to face her. It was open to an Excel sheet of funds, incoming and outgoing:

Shelter Rock's financial details, graphs, numbers—all things that bored Jacey. Things other people handled for her. So why was Dash showing her? To prove . . . what?

"You don't have to make a decision now," Dash told her. "But since it's almost Christmas . . ."

Jacey flashed on the kids at Shelter Rock, the paucity of toys, electronics, books, computers. It would be kinda cool to do a full-out Santa trip there. A smile played on her face. She could go with Desi—before everyone split for the holidays. How fun would it be to hit Best Buy, Toys "R" Us, Target, and other places like that and, wow . . . maybe a cash donation, too? She told Desi what she was thinking.

"Really?" Dash asked. "You want to do that? I mean, that'd be awesome, Your Awesomeness!"

Jacey focused on him with an intensity she hadn't realized she felt until it spilled out: "I just need to say this, Dash. I may be confused about some things—and I won't change my mind about playing Santa right now—but I know there's something you are not telling me about Shelter Rock. Something you and Desi are hiding."

With a theatrical flourish, Jacey grabbed the car keys and headed out, thinking, Good, let him chew on that for a while!

A wild and wonderful thing happened as she drove toward the shopping center, making a mental list of

165

presents for the Shelter Rock kids—Jacey Chandliss got a total brainstorm! She suddenly knew what she was giving Matt Canseco for Christmas. The one gift so perfect it surprised her she hadn't thought of it sooner.

## Jacey and Garrett–Gotcha!

She can deny it, but we've got proof: Jacey Chandliss and Garrett McKinley, judge and contestant on *Generation Next*, are seeing each other. And being seen, and photographed, by others—right out in the open. Did Jacey pick the Farmers Market for a rendezvous because she thought no one would think of finding the platinum princess at a tacky tourist trap?

Oh, think again, sweet starlet!

The hiding-in-plain-sight ruse was a bust. As in, you and Garrett are so busted! 'Cause ya got caught red-handed—dining alfresco at a table for two. We heard more than the sound of sandwiches being consumed. There were giggles, touching, and—did you really think that slanted umbrella would conceal the serious canoodling? After lunch, you shopped, sticking close together—very close. Wasn't it cute when you licked his finger? Wasn't it sweet when he shielded you from tourists? And that lip-lock: brief, but telling. Après-shopping, you hopped in your car and rode off into the sunset together.

A starlet is entitled to her flings. (As if everyone doesn't know that your erstwhile boyfriend, Matt Canseco, has his!)

But, whoa, Nelly! Aren't you a judge on the TV reality show Garrett's trying to win? If the producers don't do the right thing and kick you off, Jacey, you should step down and recuse yourself from your judging duties.

Now would be a good time.

# Chapter Thirteen

## A Starlet's Lonely Christmas

'Twas the day before Christmas, and all through the beach house, Jacey was scrambling, quick as a mouse!

She woke up with a smile on her face and a silly rhyme in her head. What a day this was going to be, and oh, what a night!

First things first. She slithered past Dash's and Desi's rooms, checking to make sure that they were still asleep, since she hadn't wrapped their presents yet and this was the last day she'd see them before they left for vacation.

She'd snagged Dash the newest iPod, best sellers by his favorite authors, an Armani silk robe, Stitches jeans, and Tod's alligator loafers. Just as she was about to place them by the tiny tree they'd bought, Jacey changed her mind. Dash and his family celebrated Christmas, but this year, Aja was in the picture, too—and he was Jewish. In a nod to that relationship, Jacey placed the gift-wrapped boxes by the menorah instead.

Shopping for Desi had been a blast. The wide-eyed girl appreciated everything; anything shiny and new excited her. For Des, Jacey had gone into Juicy Couture overload. She had bought her some sparkling cuff bracelets, a star pendant, the cutest jeans, a jacket, and a minidress. She wrapped them separately and scattered them around the tree. At Cinnamon's suggestion, she also rewarded her posse, along with everyone else on Team Jacey, with substantial cash bonuses.

Once everything was in place, Jacey stepped back and admired her handiwork. Sappy as it was, Christmas was her favorite time of year, and gift-giving was the part she loved best. How fun was it, watching the faces of her family and friends as they unwrapped her gifts?

A bit later, when she'd made enough noise to wake them, Jacey was fully rewarded by Dash's and Desi's reactions. Dash was overwhelmed by the amount of thought Jacey had put into his gifts, and he appreciated the symbolism of placing them by the menorah.

Desi was overjoyed as she ripped open each box. But she didn't burst into tears until she came to the cuffs and pendant. "You didn't! You di— Ahhhh! Just what I wanted! How'd you know?"

"Maybe because you've been leaving hints for the past few weeks?"

"I wasn't sure you'd notice."

"Who you callin' self-absorbed?" Jousting with Desi was fun.

When Desi saw the check, enclosed in a card, the real waterworks began. Sobbing and hugging Jacey, she sniffed, "You know this has been my best year ever. You didn't have to do this."

"According to her accountant, she did," smart aleck Dash put in; then he thanked her profusely for his bonus.

"With all you guys have done for me over the past year, I think we'd all agree you earned it!" Jacey exclaimed.

"What about your gifts?" Desi asked, pointing to several brightly wrapped packages with Jacey's name on them. "Aren't you gonna open them?"

"I'm a traditionalist. I think I'll wait until Christmas morning," she said. "If you guys don't mind." *'Cause that's when I'll be with Matt, and how much sweeter will that be?*

Her BFFs, who could read her mind, smirked.

"Let me see, having a straight boy sleep over, while

you're in the house alone?" Dash said, teasing her. "I don't think that's allowed. I might have to call your parents."

Jacey mock-kicked him. "I might have to call out for breakfast, unless you feel like rustling up some eggs. The starlet is hungry!"

Dash, wearing his new robe over his pj's, pretended to bow. "Of course, your Divine Hungry-ness, what was I thinking?" He headed into the kitchen.

Soon, Jacey heard the sounds of eggs scrambling in the pan—and smelled the acrid odor of burnt toast. Someone was in the kitchen with Dash. . . .

"It wasn't my fault," Desi said, defending herself. "Look at this!" Jacey came into the room just in time to see Desi hold up her BlackBerry—as if the PDA were responsible for creating the charcoal bread.

"What is it today?" Jacey heaved a sigh. "What lump of coal has the blogger decided to dump on us the day before Christmas?"

The Jaceyfan blog had not only managed to provide details on Jacey's and Garrett's Farmers Market hook-up, as the blogger called it. There were also dozens of photos.

Damn! Jacey had been so sure no one had recognized them. She hadn't even been stopped for an autograph!

Was the blogger stalking her now? That was a sickening thought. But she'd have noticed! She hadn't been that absorbed in Garrett—had she? And how could he not have realized it either? Grrrrr!

Pissed off as she was, Jacey had little time to obsess. Her to-do list was off the charts. She left Dash to handle the onslaught of calls that would certainly result from this blog entry. She and Desi had pressing business to attend to.

It was time to do the Santa thing for Shelter Rock. Jacey had spent the previous evening gleefully power-shopping, gathering gifts by the bushel. As she explained to her friends, if her life were a movie, this would have been the montage scene: quick cuts of Jacey shopping at Best Buy, Target, Toys "R" Us, and Barnes & Noble. At each stop, with the help of a VIP personal shopper, she ran her credit cards ragged, leaving a ka-chinging trail of ecstatic salespeople in her wake.

She'd snared laptops, DVDs, CDs, books, digital cameras, iPods, dolls, and games, both handheld and video, and one each of the latest PlayStation, Nintendo, Wii, and Xbox consoles.

It didn't mean, she explained to her friends, that she'd decided to appoint Shelter Rock as her only charitable cause. This was merely a goodwill gesture to make the kids' holidays a little brighter.

Mission accomplished!

The sight of their awestruck little faces, smiles, and dancing eyes when they saw Santa and his elf (yes, Desi had dressed up!) arriving not by sleigh but by SUV was a bigger payoff than Jacey could have ever imagined. The only people who knew they were coming were Rosalie Cross and her staff of volunteers. They'd decided to let Jacey surprise the kids.

Rosalie choked back tears of gratitude as volunteers unloaded the car. "Most of the kids didn't get to go home for Christmas," she said. "A few families may visit tomorrow, but now these children know they haven't been forgotten."

Desi cried. Jacey almost did. The starlet couldn't remember feeling this joyous on any Christmas, ever. And the best was yet to come.

On the way to the airport, where Jacey was depositing Desi, she asked her friend, "Wonder why the penniless Prince Jake, the director dude, wasn't there today—it being nearly Christmas."

Had Desi just tensed up? "I'm sure he'll show tomorrow morning," she said, "but no way could he make the kids happier than you did today."

It sounded reasonable, Jacey thought. Still, was it possible, Jacey wondered, that Desi knew him?

She accompanied her friend into the Northwest

Airlines terminal, where Dash and Aja awaited. After one more group hug, Jacey sent her posse on their way.

Soon, she was back behind the wheel of her Escalade, ready to begin the evening's preparations. Matt had already called her a few times, but she hadn't picked up, or listened to his messages. All she had to do was hear his voice and she'd spoil the surprise. Matt had that effect on her.

Jacey headed for Fred Segal, the boutique where she'd taken the *Gen Next* contestants. The shop had the most delicious-smelling candles. She bought a dozen. Next, she hit Arclight Records, where a pimply-faced clerk smirked when she asked for romantic CDs.

"Romantic? You mean booty-call CDs?" he had the gall to say. Jacey requested a personal shopper at once and eventually went home with the latest music from John Mayer, Michael Bublé, and Seal. Next, she hit a florist and picked up several dozen red roses.

She saved the best for last. La Perla was a sexy lingerie store like Victoria's Secret, only more high end. Jacey's dilemma once inside was which sexy lingerie to pick for her very first time.

Ordinarily, she'd have called Ivy. But Ivy had never trusted Matt, nor was she in any emotional condition to help Jacey choose teddies. Desi and Dash were on a plane, so they were out.

Nor would Jacey accept help from an oversolicitous saleswoman. After being caught with Garrett the previous day, she wouldn't put it past anyone to sneak a picture of her trying on some lacy undies and send it to the blogger.

This was all on her. What would Matt like best? A teddy? A push-up bra? A bustier? Anything in white, she admitted, would be appropriate for the occasion. But that might seem too bridey. Black felt too vampy. And she lacked the confidence to go with a G-string or a thong.

Eventually, Jacey settled on a blush-tinted lace push-up bra and matching bikini bottoms.

Jacey checked her dinner order on the ride home. The upscale supermarket Gelson's was scheduled to deliver a fully cooked turkey and all the trimmings. Her job was to warm it up in the oven. She was fairly confident she could manage.

While placing the candles around house, she heard her phone ring. Matt again.

"Soon," she whispered at the cell phone. "Soon."

She set about scattering rose petals, making a trail from the front door through the living room, up the steps to her bedroom, and onto the bed. She deliberated about the condom, though. Should she put it out on the night-stand or tuck it discreetly into a drawer? She decided on the latter.

While uncorking a bottle of wine and setting two glasses on the coffee table, she was reminded that the idea for this evening had come from Garrett.

Casting Matt in the leading-man role instead of Garrett had transformed a special evening into one in which she gave Matt the most meaningful, intimate gift she could: herself.

How surprised would he be to find her clad only in a silk robe, loosely tied at the waist? How big would his eyes get when he scoped the lacy La Perlas underneath? Would there be tears in his eyes when he realized the significance of it?

After taking a lap around the house to make sure everything was choreographed just so, Jacey went upstairs to shower and do her hair and makeup.

After she finished, she slipped into her silky under-wear and robe.

By the time the bell rang, Jacey was so excited she practically flung the door open.

That anticipatory rush of exhilaration turned to confusion almost instantly. Matt was there all right, alone and on time. He wore jeans, a beat-up leather jacket, and what could best be described as a scowl. His body was tense; his eyes flashed angrily. The door shut behind him.

Then his eyes traveled from her face to her body. That was when his jaw went slack. "Wow . . ." was all she heard. There might have been more to his sentence, but Jacey cut him off; she smothered him in kisses, then took his hands, pulled him inside, and led him over to the sofa, where she positioned herself on his lap.

She watched him take in the candles, the wine, the rose petals leading up the steps. Jacey ran her fingers through his hair, then embraced him and leaned in to smooch his neck.

Suddenly Matt jerked his head away and gave her a look that sent tremors up her spine.

"What's the matter? Am I doing something wrong?" she asked.

"Your timing," he answered gruffly. "That's what's wrong."

"It's Christmas Eve," she whispered, crossing her legs seductively. "I could have waited until the morning, but I thought my gift was something you might not want to wait for." She might have been a virgin, but Jacey's experience had taught her that guys were the ones with little patience when it came to sex. Now, however, she was confused. Why was Matt pushing her away?

"I chilled some wine," she said, slipping off his lap and pouring a glass. "Maybe you'd like some first?" She suddenly felt like the biggest dork—did she have to get him looped to be in the mood?

"No wine, Jacey. We have to talk."

Her stomach knotted up even as she tried to convince herself that Matt was probably just concerned about her. He wanted her to be sure she really wanted to do this before her eighteenth birthday. She decided to demonstrate that she was more than ready, right then and there.

"We'll have all night to talk," she said, licking her lips and undoing the sash that held the robe closed. It slid off her shoulders, exposing the push-up bra.

She'd unnerved him. He swallowed. "Do you even know what you're doing?"

"Of course not," she purred, moving closer to him and stroking his cheek. "I've never done this before. I'm making it up as I go along." Their thighs were touching. Jacey fully expected Matt to smother her in hot kisses, or just go ahead and make a move to unhook her bra.

She did not expect him to inch away from her again.

Do I have bad breath? Jacey thought in panic. Am I repelling him?

She choked back a lump in her throat and managed to sputter, "Okay, what's wrong?"

"I think you know," Matt said in a serious tone.

"All I know is I'm ready. Tonight's the night. I thought this was what you wanted, Matt."

"I did—but . . ." He trailed off.

"But what? This isn't just a make-out session. You understand, right?" She reached for him.

"You're being very clear. I understand why, too. That's the problem."

"There's a problem? I tried to make everything perfect. . . ."

"So perfect I'd forget about you and that Garrett character?" Matt's tone was steely.

Jacey's jaw dropped. "Ga—Garrett? What's he got to do this?"

"Everything, it seems to me." Matt shot her an accusing look.

She was stunned. "I don't know what you're even talking about."

"Then I'll spell it out for you," he said harshly. "You got caught with Garrett. You feel guilty, so you're trying to make it up to me with sex."

"How could you even think that?" Jacey said. "There's nothing going on with Garrett and me."

He raised his eyebrows. "Really? So you're saying the pictures aren't real?"

"The pictures?" she repeated, feeling stupid. "You mean that idiotic blog? You can't possibly believe that."

"If I wasn't sure before, I am now," Matt said. "I called you a bunch of times today. You didn't return any of my messages. So I showed up. Only to find you've staged this seduction scene. That tells me all I need to know."

"It's not staged!" Jacey bit her lip, trying her best not to cry. "It's real! My feelings for you are real."

"Well, my feelings are suspicious," Matt said. "You're the one who wanted to be exclusive. Then this dude comes along, and you forget all about that. Only, you're a teenager, so you deal with it by being immature. I knew you couldn't handle this."

The remark landed like a slap across the face. Jacey flinched. "You're wrong, Matt, about everything. Maybe something else is going on with you. 'Cause it can't be this. I bumped into him randomly. . . . I was shopping for a present for you! Garrett even gave me this idea—" She stopped suddenly, realizing how that sounded.

"He gave you the idea, huh? Did he offer to practice with you first?" Matt stood now, looking down at her, and Jacey felt small and very vulnerable. With considerable effort, she retied the sash of the robe and composed herself.

"Please don't be like that, Matt. Don't make a friendly shopping trip into something way more than it was."

"Yeah, friendly. You two seemed very friendly. Snuggling, kissing, walking so close you were touching. Licking his finger! The least you could have done was let me know before the rest of the world did."

"We weren't snuggling!" Jacey exclaimed. "He kissed me on the cheek to thank me, and I accidentally turned my head. And do you have any idea how crowded that place was? We had to hold on to each other, or—"

"You'd lose him in the crowd?" Matt said sarcastically.

"Matt, please. How can I prove that I don't want Garrett?" Jacey worked to keep her voice as reasonable and calm as possible.

"You already proved that you do," Matt snorted. "For weeks, you've been telling me you need to wait. Then you get caught with him, and suddenly, you're ready for sex with me? Just like that?"

"Do you want to accuse me, or talk to me?" she asked. "Because if you're using this bogus accusation to get out of . . . being with me . . . just say it."

"Maybe you're the one realizing you're in over your head," he shot back. "And this is your way of telling me."

"This is nuts!" she cried. "I'm more into you than ever!

I was shopping for a present; I couldn't find anything, until I realized that what I really wanted to give you was the most important, most personal, most loving gift that I, as a girl, could give a guy. Myself."

"That's a nice speech, Jacey. And on some level, I'm sure you think it's true. I don't."

Jacey couldn't believe she was hearing this. "You're jealous! How can you be jealous of something that isn't real?"

"I'm not jealous, Jacey. I don't get jealous. I don't appreciate being played. And personally, I think you lost your grip on what's real the day you won *Generation Next*."

"Why are you doing this?" she demanded, the tears flowing freely. "Why are you hurting me over what's in some stupid blog?"

"I think that in the who-hurt-who olympics, you get the gold. First you blab your attraction to him on national TV. Now there are pictures to prove you acted on it. So don't accuse me of hurting you."

"But . . . but . . . I would never hurt you."

"No, huh? You know how it feels to look like a sucker? Everyone reads the tabloids. Everyone sees the pictures, and they believe what they see."

"*Everyone* reads them. *You're* not supposed to believe them. You're supposed to know better," she whispered to his back as he turned away from her and walked out the door.

And Jacey Chandliss, multimillionaire starlet, pixie-dust girl in sunny Malibu, couldn't stop shivering, encased as she was in the icy chill of abandonment.

# Chapter Fourteen

## Jacey and Ivy—The Heartbreak Tour: L.V., SoBe, NYC-Ya-Later!

Stunned and confused, Jacey drifted through the house, robotically extinguishing candles, sweeping dozens of rose petals into a dustpan and dumping them into the garbage. She poured the wine down the drain, shoved the bottles into the recycling bin. The entire turkey got tossed into the trash along with John Mayer, Michael Bublé, and Seal, which were no longer music to her ears.

When there was nothing left to do, Jacey made a phone call.

"Are you sure?" Cinnamon kept asking. Jacey's agent refused to believe that her star client had impulsively changed her holiday plans for no apparent reason.

"I want to go to all the parties we've been invited to that are happening between Christmas and New Year's Day—as long as they aren't in Los Angeles," Jacey instructed Cinnamon. "I need to get out of this town."

Cinnamon resisted at first, but eventually agreed that a jet-setting, high-profile Jacey was good publicity for the upcoming *Supergirl*. "But I don't like the idea of you going alone. You're still underage. Who can you get to come along?"

"I don't need company, I need to party!" Jacey sobbed into the phone. That was the first time she had cried since Matt slammed the door on her, and on them.

Two days later, Jacey got exactly what she'd asked for. Clad in an adorable white miniskirt and chic dancing boots, she was having a blast at the swanky Las Vegas nightclub Body English. She wasn't alone.

She'd called Ivy from the air, selling her a week of power-shopping and party-hopping. "In places where it's warm," she'd added, in case Ivy needed the extra incentive.

She didn't have to ask twice. Ives, nursing her own wounds, was all about enabling. She'd been home in Michigan for over a week, and had had just about enough of family time in the cold clime. Ivy arrived in Las Vegas the day after Christmas, and the cousins wasted no time puttin' a hurtin' on the designer boutiques lining the marble corridors of the Bellagio resort hotel.

They needed a lot of stuff. There were multiple parties to attend, and Jacey had absolutely nothing to wear. She'd fled Los Angeles without even a suitcase. As for Ivy, nothing said, "Buh-bye, Emilio; hello, excess and entitlement" better than an ultimate shopping spree in which everything was free (courtesy of Jacey). Besides, partying hearty was an excellent elixir for their broken hearts.

It had been almost too easy. The call to Cinnamon had netted immediate action. The studio had put a private plane at Jacey's disposal for the entire week, to whisk her away at will, as long as she chose places where glitz and glam ruled and photographers were there to cover it.

All Jacey had to do was flash her smile to get recognized—it bought her immediate entrée into every worthwhile party in town. She and Ivy started at Body English at the Hard Rock Hotel, a must-be-seen-at nightclub for musicians, socialites, and other Hollywood types. Translation: only the famous and financially fortunate should even think of getting in.

Commandeering a primo spot on the upper level of the multitiered club and looking down on the dance floor, the cousins made a dynamic duo: one tall, dark, and dramatic, the other, curvy, fair, and famous—Betty and Veronica for the MySpace generation. Jacey provided the star power; hers was the beautiful face everyone knew and clamored to be photographed with. Her flashy, green-eyed friend, wearing a short Zac Posen mini and high heels, was the girl every guy in the room *wanted* to know. And not just for a photo op.

Take that, Emilio! Jacey thought, as gorgeous guys flocked to them. Meanwhile, she multitasked. Wine spritzers kept her happy, but not looped, as she did kissy-face with a string of celebs and rockers.

A photographer from *the* exclusive *Las Vegas Magazine* snapped pictures of Jacey and Ivy posing with all of them, as well as with practiced socialite scenesters like Ivanka and Eric Trump, who turned out to be funny, smart, and charming. Who knew?

Jacey deliberately did not pose alone with any guys, however. If there was even one live ember left between her and Matt, she wasn't going to risk dousing it.

Which didn't mean she couldn't flirt with the steady stream of studs she and Ivy were attracting. Like the brown-eyed, curly-haired cutie currently tapping her on the shoulder and extending his (manicured, as she couldn't help noting) hand.

"You're Jacey Chandliss," he said, with a confident but

friendly smile. "I hope I'm not interrupting. I wanted to introduce myself. I'm Ted Lyons, from the Wynn Las Vegas."

"Nice to meet you, Ted-from-the-Wynn," Jacey said, shaking his hand.

"Is this your first time in Las Vegas?" Ted asked.

"Let's just say this is the first time I've been here intending to have a blast," Jacey replied.

"A worthy goal. May I help you achieve it?" Ted offered.

In seconds, Jacey was in the middle of the dance floor, gyrating to Beyoncé's "Irreplaceable" and Justin Timberlake's "Sexyback." Ted-from-the-Wynn proved an excellent dance partner.

"So, what do you do at the Wynn?" Jacey asked. She knew it was one of the newest, glitziest, most high-rolling resorts on the Las Vegas Strip and assumed Ted was a pool boy or bartender.

"I'm actually part owner," he said without skipping a beat.

Ted impressed Jacey, mostly because he was a rich boy who wasn't a jerk.

Jacey relaxed and lost herself in the music—until DJ AM, the famous house spinner at Body English, played Shakira's classic "Hips Don't Lie." It felt like a stealth attack. Jacey's memory was jolted right back to the last time she'd been dancing in Las Vegas. What a buzz kill.

Even a starlet could do the math. She'd fled to Sin City two times, both involving Matt Canseco. And sex. That first time, she'd caught him with Carlin; her heart had been broken. Now, he'd jilted her—mistakenly believing she'd tried to break his. Maybe Ivy and Cinnamon, the prime folks who'd warned her not to get involved with Matt, had been right after all: Matt Canseco and Jacey Chandliss were like fire and ice, oil and water. They didn't mix well and never would. She hadn't listened. Why? Was it because pampered princesses got what they wanted whether it was good for them or not?

Damn. Just thinking about him was enough to make her check her phone. Alas, Matt had not, in fact, tried to reach her. Worse, she looked up to find Ivy staring down at her.

"No, no, no," Ivy cautioned, waving a finger at Jacey. "We're not thinking about the losers we left in L.A. No rearview mirrors tonight. We're fully focused on shiny new playthings right here. Got it?"

Jacey, who had yet to tell Ivy the details of the Christmas Eve debacle, gave her cousin a doleful look, but Ivy ignored it and dragged her back onto the dance floor, where they found Ted and one of his friends: a tall, buff looker named Zack.

The foursome clicked instantly and decided to leave Body English for Tryst, the club at Ted's hotel, where more fun and fabulosity awaited. For the next few laughing, dancing, and glass-clinking hours, Jacey was able to shed her Matt obsession.

It turned out that Ted's mom was a major stockholder in the Wynn and other hotels on the Vegas Strip, vaulting the curly-topped cutie to the Vegas A-list. Zack, who attended UNLV, had been his best bud since grade school.

By the time the guys dropped Ivy and Jacey off at their hotel, it was after three in the morning. The foursome agreed to see one another the following night.

"Methinks me likey Zacky," declared Ivy, who was feeling no pain.

"Enough to . . ."—Jacey paused—"make tomorrow night memorable?"

Ivy smiled wickedly. "Nighty-night, li'l . . ." She burped loudly. ". . . Cuz."

The following night Ivy made good on her implied promise. After hitting the swanky nightclub Tao at the Venetian and the poolside lounge Skin at the Palms, Ted suggested going to a private party at his friend's house. The house, as Jacey ought to have guessed, was in fact an amazing mansion with a manmade lake, private tennis courts, and of course, an open bar around which Las Vegas's young, beautiful, rich, and hip congregated.

They'd been there less than a half hour when a fully soused Ivy disappeared with Zack, "to see the upstairs," as she called out to Jacey.

"I think they've hit it off," Ted remarked.

"Yup," Jacey agreed. "I also think they'll be checking out the upstairs awhile."

Ted laughed and offered to show Jacey around the rest of the mansion. When he stopped to talk to one of his friends, Jacey excused herself, indicating that she was going to the ladies' room. Instead, she found a quiet spot in which to check her voice mail and text messages.

She had several, from Desi, Dash, her parents, Cinnamon, and Peyton.

"Who is he?"

Jacey whirled around. Ted had come up behind her. She flushed. "Who's who?"

"This is the fourth time tonight you've snuck away to check your messages," Ted pointed out.

"You counted?" Jacey was surprised.

"When I'm attracted to a girl, I observe."

Jacey blushed, feeling both complimented and caught in the act.

"Whoever he is," Ted said with a resigned sigh, "he's stupid for not being with you."

When Ivy's evening ended up being a bust—the Zack hook-up that wasn't—the cousins were ready for their next party destination. They landed in SoBe—South Beach, Florida—on December twenty-eighth and checked in to the deluxe Delano hotel. Room service provided a hairdresser and makeup artist. Then it was off to designer row for some shiny new outfits. Partly because they wanted to travel light, but mainly because they could, Jacey and Ivy had arranged for all the clothes they had bought in Las Vegas—and worn once!—to be donated to the worthy Clothes Off Our Back charity.

"I always used to wonder," Ivy mused, "how it was even possible for stars to be in a city partying one night, then suddenly show up in another the next, looking completely refreshed and dressed to kill."

"Now we know!" Jacey high-fived her cousin. "It's all about private planes and unlimited credit cards."

"And don't forget celebrity," Ivy pointed out. "Famous people can snap their fingers and get pretty much anything they want, any time."

Anything, Jacey thought, but love. She mentally kicked herself. Queen of clichés much?

As Jacey tried on a strapless red cocktail-length bubble-hemmed dress, Ivy asked, "Do you . . . ever feel guilty?"

The dress fit perfectly. "About all this? Living this lifestyle, having all these mind-bending experiences?" Jacey asked.

Ivy nodded. "It's not something either of us ever dreamed of, back in Michigan. At least, I didn't."

"I did for a while—feel guilty, that is," Jacey admitted. "And then I read an interview with Rosie O'Donnell."

Ivy's eyebrows arched. "Do tell."

"I don't remember the exact quote, but when she made some list with other superwealthy women, she said something like, the only reason people have too much money is because they don't give enough away. You have a responsibility to spread the wealth around, to use it to help others. I thought that was pretty cool."

"How very self-sacrificing," Ivy said.

"It's easy to mock stars like Angelina and Madonna," Jacey said, deciding which pair of shoes would go best with the dress, "but they do spend gazillions for good causes."

"Your new role models?" Ivy was teasing, but Jacey was actually serious.

"Maybe. It's something I could feel good about doing." Jacey twirled in the dress, watching herself in the mirror. Yeah, this'd be tonight's style statement, she thought.

"Are you going to support Shelter Rock?" Ivy asked, slipping into a pair of strappy silver sandals.

Jacey frowned. "I'd like to, but there's something fishy about it."

"You think it's bogus?"

"Not Shelter Rock itself. Dash checked it out. But there's something unkosher about the way Desi just happened to find it, and how she's pressuring me to get involved. She's hiding something from me. Dash, too."

"I agree that Dash may be good at subterfuge," Ivy noted. "But Des? Can't keep a secret to save her cute little life. You'll find out soon enough."

Miami felt like Las Vegas East, except with humidity. The nightclub scene here involved more poolside bashes, and the magazine snapping their photos was called *Ocean Drive*. The A-listers were a completely different subspecies of the familiar celebs found in Hollywood and Las Vegas.

"They're like this otherworldly race of perfectly tanned and toned creatures," Ivy said while reading an article. "They prey on other people's self-esteem. They're called SoBeans."

"If our self-esteem drops below Gisele Bündchen level, we split. That's all." With a twist of the wrist, Jacey did a dead-on imitation of Meryl Streep in *The Devil Wears Prada*.

She was, of course, covering up. Without Ivy's knowledge, she'd been swallowing her pride, texting Matt every day. (For example: *How can u believe gossip & rumors? How could u not trust me? Please let's talk. Write back, or call.*)

Matt did neither.

That night, Jacey partied harder than she had in Las Vegas. Her famous face got her into every happening party, and she and Ivy rubbed spray-on tanned elbows with the likes of J.Lo, Diddy, and even Donatella Versace. Awards season was coming up, and Jacey wondered if the designer might offer to dress her for any of the parties.

She didn't.

Two days later, Jacey and Ivy summoned the jet and headed north to New York City, where they intended to spend the last two days of the year. High above the east coast of the U.S., Ivy broached "the subject," without preamble.

"Who was it this time? Please don't tell me Carlin again!"

"Completely wrong," Jacey responded with a sigh.

"Unless," Ivy snarled, "Emilio decided to share Double D's."

"Wrong again," Jacey replied. "Matt walked out on me because he thinks I cheated on him."

"No way!" Ivy exclaimed. "Who does he think you hooked up with?"

"According to the blog—" Jacey began.

"The blog? Who believes what that idiot writes?" Ivy paused. "Unless . . . are you?"

"Am I what?"

"With Garrett?"

"And this is why I haven't wanted to talk about it with you," Jacey groused. "Because it's not even a conversation."

Ivy gulped. "Cuz, I'm really sorry. I'm no fan of Matt's, but this is a new one. It's too stupid to even talk about, let alone break up over. Want me to call him?"

"And say what? You were in Michigan the day I supposedly cheated with Garrett," Jacey replied.

Ivy pressed her lips together. "I take it he hasn't called you."

"Nope. Or answered my calls or texts."

"Then stop calling," Ivy declared. "He's the one who messed up. Not you. You have nothing to apologize for."

Maybe I do, Jacey thought, as Ivy closed her eyes for

an airborne snooze. Maybe I should apologize for missing all the signs, for being too absorbed in my fantasy even to answer the phone that day. I should have known why he was so mad. Maybe I could have diffused the bomb, instead of letting it blow up in my face. Would some older, more experienced girl have handled it better?

New York City, the last stop on the Jacey-and-Ivy-broken-hearts tour, instantly provided something else to deal with: not freezing their butts off! The cousins bought ski jackets at the airport and then, directly after checking into the swank Soho Grand Hotel, dashed to Prada, A/X, Armani, and Bloomingdale's to stock up on cashmere sweaters, Tracey Ross mukluks, and cozy coats.

Ivy called Cinnamon and Peyton, and by evening, she and Jacey had invites to hot spots such as Butter, the Buddha Bar, and Tenjune.

Jacey had a good feeling about the New York club scene.

It turned out that Jacey would never make a living as a psychic.

### Jacey Jet-Sets, Matt Mixes It Up

While Jacey's busy bouncing between Las Vegas, South Beach, and New York, her boyfriend—is he still her boyfriend?—has been having himself a merry little Christmas, Matt Canseco style! Matt's been spotted bumper-to-bumper bar-hopping, flirting with anything in a skirt, getting happily hammered, and true to his rep, leaving trashed-up messes and battle-scarred bruisers (meaning: anyone he picks a fight with) in his wake. Say this for macho Matt: at least he pays for his messes, always leaving plenty of money for the cleanup bills. I guess there's some kind of honor among rage-a-holics.

# Chapter Fifteen

## The Boyfriend-Go-Round

Check that. Club-hopping in New York might have been fantastically fresh, only, by early evening, Jacey found out she'd have to go it alone. She and Ivy were glammed up, warmed up, and glitzed to go when Ivy got the call.

Jacey didn't have to ask: shock and awe had staged a coup on Ivy's beautiful face as her willowy cousin read the caller ID.

Emilio.

In spite of everything, Ivy was going to take the call.

Their two-bedroom suite at the Soho Grand Hotel provided Ivy with plenty of privacy. Jacey sensed that her cousin was going to be on the phone for a long time. So she flipped on the TV, put her feet up on the bed, and ordered room service.

By the time *Grey's Anatomy* came on, Jacey knew they probably weren't going to Butter, or anywhere else that night.

Not together, anyway.

Ivy finally reappeared. Her glowing, tearstained face told the story. Emilio must have begged his way back into her heart. Jacey scooched over on the king-size bed, and Ivy plopped down. While picking through the french fries brought up by room service, Ivy recounted their conversation.

"Emilio said he'd never messed up so badly in his life. He's not that guy—some uncaring jerk who treats girl-friends like that. But he said it's always been different with me. He told me . . ."—Ivy sniffed, then reached for a tissue to dry her eyes—"that he's always loved me. And when I got the internship, he got scared."

"Scared of what?" Jacey asked, supremely skeptical about Emilio's sincerity.

"That'd I get to be this big, important power agent and wouldn't want to be seen with him. He already felt like he had to make an appointment to see me."

"Why couldn't he tell you that before hooking up with Double-D's?" Jacey asked. It seemed like a reasonable question.

Ivy didn't have an answer. "He said that all these weeks away from me he's been empty inside—"

Jacey's jaw dropped. Emilio had been acting more than fulfilled making out in the *Generation Next* audience. She wanted to point that out, but was deep in diplomatic mode.

Ivy continued, "He realizes now that he has to take a chance. If I still want to be with him." She laughed ruefully. "He said he wouldn't care even if I get so busy that I work day and night, even if I wear designer suits and have a Bluetooth in my ear in bed. He can't face being without me."

Jacey swallowed. "That's a sweet speech, Ives, but are you sure you can trust him?"

"No, Jace, I'm not sure. And I won't be, from three thousand miles away. I've got to go back."

Jacey didn't believe one word of squirmy Emilio's take-me-back speech. But Ivy's voice left no doubt. She was leaving for Los Angeles, immediately.

"I'll call for the plane," Jacey said. "And I'll ride to the airport with you."

"You won't come with?" Ivy said hopefully. "I feel like I'm abandoning you."

"You could never abandon me, Cuz," Jacey reassured her. "I'm not ready to go back. It's almost New Year's Eve, and I'd rather spend it here than so close to someone who doesn't want to see me."

Ivy had tears in her eyes again. "It's all so bizarre; I feel so strange. I pushed myself to believe it was over, but a part of me always hoped he'd come back."

"Is that why the Zack thing was a bust?" Jacey asked speculatively.

"I thought I'd be a stronger person," said Ivy, eyeing Jacey meaningfully. "Here I am telling you not to call Matt. Meanwhile, I run back the minute Emilio summons me. I'm sorry."

"Don't put yourself down, Ives. You can't help who you fall in love with. All we can do is hope it lasts this time."

"How'd you get so wise, little cousin?"

"It's in the genes?" Jacey guessed. "Maybe we're both a little reckless, ruled by our hearts. Impulsive. Hopeful."

Ivy hugged her tightly. "I can't stand the thought of you alone here."

"I won't be alone," Jacey said with more conviction than she felt. "There's always HBO if I can't find a friendly, trustworthy soul to party with."

"Promise me you won't go clubbing by yourself. You're only seventeen."

"Almost eighteen. I don't need a babysitter twenty-four-seven. Anyway, I think I remember Adam Pratt saying he'd be in town. I'm sure he'd love to hang with me, especially if there are cameras around. I'll see you in a few days. Just remember to send the plane back for me!"

"Are you sure? Are you positive?" Ivy asked again.

"I insist," Jacey said. "Just don't let Emilio step on your heart again. If he does, he'll have me—and the whole posse—to answer to."

Jacey sort of did what she'd promised Ivy. She called a friend.

Garrett picked up on the first ring. "Jacey!" He sounded really happy to hear from her. "Merry Christmas! How are you?"

"Great!" she lied. "And guess what? I'm not that far from you."

Garrett was taken by surprise. Jacey had said she'd be spending the holidays in Los Angeles. She explained that Ivy had been unexpectedly called back to the West Coast, and Garrett was the only person she knew in New York.

"New York is a big state," Garrett said. "I'd love to come to town and hang out with you, but I'm over two hours away. I don't see how it could work."

Was he truly disappointed, or relieved? "I have a limo at my disposal, paid for by the studio. How 'bout if I send it for you?" Jacey asked temptingly.

Jacey replayed the conversation in her head while getting ready for Garrett to arrive. He hadn't needed much cajoling. He admitted that he'd always been fascinated by the club scene—what he'd read about it, anyway. He had never thought of himself as someone who'd ever get past a bouncer.

"Stick with me, kid," Jacey cracked. "You'll get into every club in town."

But would he fit in? Garrett worried that he'd stick out like a country bumpkin in a crowd of city slickers.

"Don't wear overalls," Jacey deadpanned. "Besides, you're forgetting something: your own celebrity star is rising. You're one of two finalists on *Generation Next*. Trust me, being almost famous counts."

"What if we get photographed together?" Garrett asked, though he'd already caved. "Won't it look bad for you? You really got hammered after the Farmers Market."

Thanks for reminding me, Jacey thought. She felt more than a twinge of sadness, but Garrett didn't need to know that Matt had believed the story. She breezily assured him that getting photographed together was no big deal. No one she really cared about believed that a photo of two people together made romance rumors true. *No one she cared about.*

It was close to eleven when the limo delivered Garrett

to the Soho Grand, and Jacey's heart nearly stopped when she saw him. Not fit in? Was he kidding? He looked like a Gap ad: sandy hair just scruffy enough to be cool, open sport jacket over layered sweatshirts, black jeans, and boots. All this boy needed was a starlet on his arm, and he'd be good to go.

They hit Butter first. "This is the club that Ashley Olsen's ex-boyfriend used to own," Jacey told Garrett, as the bouncer recognized her and waved them through.

It tickled her to watch Garrett's eyes go wide, not believing what was happening. His first time in an elite club and he was cutting the line, the cover charge was being waived, and a free Stella Artois beer was instantly placed in his hand.

"I want to pay for this," he said, taking a slug.

"Your money's no good," said Jacey. "Neither is mine. We get comped everywhere we go. As long as we let the photographers snap us, we're giving the club publicity. That's why they love having famous faces in places like this."

"Wow, this is so cool. I get to be treated like a star, all because I'm with you!"

"Soon you won't need me, Garrett," Jacey remarked. "When you win—obviously, I meant, *if* you win—the world will be at your feet."

"I hope you can show me which doors to walk through

and which to avoid," Garrett said seriously.

Jacey smiled, linked her arm through his, looked into his blue, blue eyes and said, "Count on it."

He grinned. "I guess you don't get carded, either."

"Not so far," Jacey said. (That might have been because Ivy had ordered the drinks for her in Las Vegas and Miami.) "Hopefully, my luck will hold." She clinked bottles with him. "Here's to a fun night!'

As they talked, Garrett took in the whole scene: cedar-plank walls without windows; cavernous, vaulted ceiling; stars and models everywhere one looked. "This place is so cool! I've never been anywhere like it."

Jacey had been everywhere like it, especially in the last five days. The clubs were all starting to blend together, diluting her appreciation for any one of them. Well, if she couldn't get excited about a hot club, at least she could have fun with the company she was keeping.

Jacey got into her role of teacher and tour guide, pointing out and introducing him to various celebrities. Garrett was a dream student, completely in awe of everything. He wasn't a bad date, either. He was easy to talk to, and he could dance. Mindful of his manners, he remembered to thank her for helping with the Christmas presents for his family. They had loved everything, he told her.

Garrett wasn't too hard on the eyes, either. More than

one slinky model type in thigh-grazing hemlines managed to "bump" into him, or simply came up to him and smiled.

"They are so hitting on you!" Jacey laughed. "You'll need to get used to this if you win."

"It's only because I'm with you that anyone is even noticing me," Garrett said.

"You're being too modest. But it is true that winning will totally upend your life."

"Not sure I'm ready for that," Garrett admitted.

Then get ready, Jacey thought, as a photographer got in their faces. Jacey posed, then pulled Garrett out onto the dance floor.

Between dances, noshes, drinks, and laughter, Jacey forgot that she wasn't supposed to talk to Garrett about *Generation Next*. Feeling flush, confident, sexy yet safe, she went ahead and asked if he'd decided what scenes he'd be doing in the finals.

"I'm not completely set," he confessed, which left the door wide open for Jacey to coach him.

That one, she walked right though.

They'd already left Butter for Buddha Bar and had had their pictures taken outside on the sidewalk.

"What are you thinking of doing?" Jacey asked, sipping an apple-flavored cocktail.

For his first appearance, Garrett was toying with either teaming up with Crystal to do a scene from the The *Outsiders* or doing a soliloquy from *Hamlet* .

For the final scene, he was thinking about something classic, like *The Count of Monte Cristo*, or going the other way entirely, maybe with something from a zany Jack Black movie.

Jacey considered. She was edging toward tipsy but was pretty sure she could think straight. "Don't do *Hamlet*," she counseled. "You've already done Shakespeare, and you blew the judges away. I think you need to show range in this last round."

"*The Outsiders,* then? I was thinking of a Dallas-and-Cherry scene, probably the one where he thinks he's the ultimate cool dude and she throws a soda at him."

"I like it—do the scene with Crystal," Jacey said. "It's risky but it'll buy you votes. You'll come across as generous, like you're giving her another chance to shine. And you can be sure she won't outshine you! I'd go with the comic piece in the end. They won't expect it from you."

"Leave 'em laughing?" Garrett asked.

"People like to laugh."

Impulsively, she kissed his cheek. And unsurprisingly, a cameraman caught it.

Oh, well, she thought, Matt thinks it's true anyway. What more damage can I do?

She slipped her arm around Garrett's waist, pulled herself close to him, and smiled for the cameras.

Suddenly, she had a brainstorm. "Want me to go over some lines with you? I totally know every word of *The Outsiders*. It won't be cheating."

"I don't know," Garrett said. "I think it's bad enough we're getting photographed together. What if someone realizes you're coaching me?"

"So, let's make sure no one sees us." Jacey was feeling reckless. She grabbed his hand.

The limo drove them to New York's once-grungy, now trendy meatpacking district, where the bartender at the intimate underground lounge Tenjune welcomed them with an on-the-house round of the club signature cocktail, p.i.n.k. vodka infused with an energy drink. It sounded pretty rank to Jacey, but turned out to be quite lovely.

So lovely she ordered another.

They skirted the crowded dance floor and found a more private spot that offered purple banquettes set against a white marble fireplace. There, the club's manager showed them to a VIP booth. Jacey slipped in on one side, assuming Garrett would sit across from her.

"A romantic setting," noted Garrett, as he slid in right next to her instead.

"It is," Jacey agreed. "And—bonus—it's quiet enough for me to rehearse with you."

"I don't think," Garrett said, moving very close, "that I even told you how amazing you look tonight."

A little nervous at his nearness, Jacey still accepted the compliment. She did like the low-cut purple halter-top dress she was wearing. It brought out the color of her eyes and, she thought, made her look taller.

"Okay," Jacey said, sipping her drink. "Let's get started." She began to recite one of Cherry's lines. She knew them by heart, not only from junior high school, where she'd read the novel, but also from having nearly performed a scene from *The Outsiders* during her own *Gen Next* tryout.

She finished her line, but Garrett missed his cue. Make that: Garrett took another cue altogether. Jacey suddenly found herself wrapped in his arms and on the receiving end of a long, lush kiss.

She pulled away, but not immediately. "I thought we were going to rehearse. For real," she heard herself stammer.

Garrett eyed her quizzically. "Sorry. Maybe I misinterpreted. You're just being a real friend. I got carried away."

Jacey started again, and this time, they did the entire

scene. Only now, Jacey was having trouble concentrating. She felt fuzzy. She had not hated his kiss. And before she could stop it, a lyric from an old song popped into her head: *If you can't be with the one you love, love the one you're with.*

After a few more drinks, coupled with alternative readings of the same scene, the club's manager materialized, informing them that they were closing for the night.

"What time is it?" Jacey asked woozily. "Didn't we just get here?"

It was four in the morning. Garrett pumped his arm in the air. "Cool! I never closed down a club in my life. Go, us!"

Jacey's intention was to have the limo drop her at her hotel, then take Garrett back home.

But Garrett had other intentions. When he started to make out with her in the back of the car, she told herself she knew what she was doing, that she could stop at any time. She didn't push him away as he untied her halter top. And when they got to the Soho Grand, and he asked if he could come up to her room, she didn't say no.

Why? She was tipsy, maybe even woozy, but not out-of-it drunk. She was lonely, but not desperate or anything. She was heartbroken over Matt, but she wasn't out for revenge. Was she?

In the elevator, Garrett stroked her face, her hair,

kissed her passionately. How ironic, Jacey thought. What if she actually wound up proving Matt right? Did she even have anything to lose? In the privacy of the hotel, who would know?

She would.

Which was why, at the last moment, when they were already on the king-size bed, half undressed and making out like crazy, she hit the brakes and pulled away.

"What's the matter?" Garrett asked breathlessly. "Why are you stopping?"

"I can't. . . ." She rolled onto her side, turning her back to him. That made it easier, somehow, to lie. "If anyone finds out, this will kill your chances of winning. You'll get booted off the show. Your dreams will be crushed."

"Who's gonna find out?" Garrett asked, echoing her own thoughts of only moments before as he stroked her bare shoulder.

"Chauffeurs talk, bellhops. They get paid for this kind of info. Anyone could have taken a cell-phone photo of us going in the elevator together." Jacey was mumbling into the pillow, convincing neither Garrett nor herself.

"If that's your real reason," he said, nuzzling her neck and sending chills down her spine, "I'm willing to take the risk. It's my future at stake here."

Jacey's body said, *Do it*. Even her brain gave her the

go-ahead. But her heart wasn't getting the memo.

"I couldn't live with myself if you lost because of one night," she whispered. "You saw how amazing your life will be if—no, when—you win. You'll get paid for doing what you love—acting—and you'll live like a prince. We shouldn't blow your chances."

"Too late," Garrett said, running his fingers down her side and over her hips. "If we're being followed, they've already got all the proof they need. If we stop now, we're only shortchanging ourselves."

"I'm sorry, Garrett."

"Look, Jacey, I figured this for a booty call. Why else would you send for me? Nothing that's happened tonight showed me anything different. Until now."

"I can't do it," she said, tearing up for real. "It's not that I'm not into you. The whole world knows what I think. I know how I feel. You're sexy, you're sweet, you're an amazing kisser. . . ." She trailed off.

"I get it now. This has nothing to do with me or *Generation Next*." Garrett turned away and sat straight up in the bed. "This is about Matt."

That was all it took, the mention of his name. Jacey burst into tears. Garrett melted. He took her in his arms and stroked her hair. "It's okay, Jacey. You love him. Go back and tell him."

"He won't listen. Garrett, he believed the blog! He walked out on me. That's why I'm here. And after he sees the photos from tonight, I've blown any chance I had. I messed up and dragged you into it."

"Did you say you had a private plane?" Garrett asked.

"Ivy's on it," she sniffed. "It's not coming back until tomorrow."

"Then here's what we do." Garrett's voice was soft, sweet, and firm. He was taking charge, and Jacey was so, so grateful. "We make sure you get some sleep. I'll stay, but I'll be in Ivy's room. We call the plane, make sure it's ready to take you back to L.A. first thing in the morning. Then, we get the limo to drive me home."

"Are you sure? I think I screwed up everything," she wailed.

"You need to go back, Jacey; you need to make that boy hear you."

# Chapter Sixteen

## The First Time

The trip to Los Angeles felt interminable. Just before they took off, Jacey texted Matt saying that she was on her way back and *really* needed to see him. After pressing SEND, she stared at her screen for a while, hoping for an instant response. There was none.

She tried to relax and read the latest *In Style* magazine, but she couldn't focus. Her mind kept wandering.

Going back and swallowing her pride (if she had any left) had made perfect sense at five in the morning. Garrett had been so convincing, so sure she could turn things around with Matt. Now, somewhere over Michigan, Jacey had her doubts. Maybe she ought to have waited a few more days, until after New Year's, or at least until Desi and Dash were back.

Jacey looked out the window and waved down at her family—as if they could have seen her and waved back. She hadn't told them the real reason she'd scrapped her original holiday plans. Instead, she had sorta lied and said that she and Ivy had decided to do some publicity for *Galaxy Rangers*.

She'd be seeing her family soon. Her mom's due date was a short six weeks away, and Jacey hoped to hang out with them for a while. Between her screwed-up love life, stinky movie, hurtful reviews, and the week of whirlwind partying she'd just had, Jacey'd had enough of the emotional roller coaster. A dose of home sounded so good just then she was almost tempted to ask the pilot to land at the Detroit airport now. She'd be safe at home, loved unconditionally, and, for a change, not the center of attention. A new baby brother was on the way, and Jacey could barely wait to welcome him.

Picturing home must have lulled Jacey to sleep, because the next thing she heard was the announcement that they'd be landing in California momentarily.

A look at her watch confirmed that five and a half hours had indeed passed. It'd be afternoon in L.A. Matt would have to have seen her message by now. How had he reacted—if at all? She tried to force herself to believe that it would be all right even if he chose silence. She'd be fine. Eventually.

Jacey drew a deep breath and flipped open her phone. One new message from Maca86. Its content was neither what she'd been hoping for nor what she'd dreaded. Matt's text message was simply confusing.

*Coming to New York. Wait for me.*

Huh? Had he not understood that she was winging her way west? She reread it, then checked the time he'd written it: just after seven in the morning, Los Angeles time, which translated to ten in the morning in New York. If she was calculating correctly, it was roughly the same time she'd sent her message.

Jacey speed-dialed Matt, but his voice mail picked up before even one ring. His phone was turned off.

Could this really be happening? She was on her way to see him just as he hopped a plane to see her? And what, they'd passed in the sky? That would be just too crazy, even for her nutty life.

Jacey was almost in Malibu when she called Ivy.

"Did he get there yet?" Ivy asked before Jacey could say a word.

"Wouldn't know."

Silence. Then. "Did you get Matt's message?" Ivy's tone had turned wary.

"Just read it now," Jacey confirmed. The car pulled into the beach house driveway.

"Jacey, where are you?"

"Open the door."

"I do not believe this!" Ivy exclaimed. "Matt was coming to New York to make up with you. Why didn't you wait for him?"

Jacey closed her eyes and wearily sank onto the couch. "Why do you think, Ives? I was doing the same exact thing. I texted him, called him, but got no response."

Ivy's slim hand flew to her mouth. "Because he was already on the way. Neither of you got the other's message in time?"

"Maybe it's a sign," Jacey said. "There's too much drama. Maybe we're just not meant to be together."

"Don't be crazy," Ivy said, brushing her off. "It's a mix-up, not an omen. I'll go check when his plane is supposed to land and book him on the next one back."

Over tea and toast, which was all Jacey's jumpy stomach could handle, Ivy filled her in on the events of the past thirty-six hours. She and Emilio had reconnected. They had approached Matt together.

"I told you not to get involved!" Jacey said.

"You should have seen him, Jace. The boy was hangdog-miserable." Emilio had revealed to Ivy that Matt had been bouncing between depression and rage all week. If he wasn't holed up in his room with iPod buds in his ears, he was at dive bars, drinking and picking fights.

Jacey had pictured Matt spending the week deleting her messages and having multiple hook-ups.

"I saw some stuff in the blog about Matt and those girls, Carlin, Kia, and the others—not true?" she ventured.

"Did you just hear yourself, Jacey? You're doing exactly what he did—believing the blog! And you're being just as ridiculous."

"Ridiculous" did not come close to describing Jacey's feelings of shame.

"Don't you get it? Matt spent the week in self-destruct mode. He had to be stopped," Ivy concluded. "For his own good."

"What'd you tell him?" Jacey asked.

"The truth. You're confused and heartbroken and have no idea why he would believe the blog over you. You don't have any feelings for Garrett McKinley; you never did."

It was not the moment to contradict her cousin.


Math had never been Jacey's best subject. All through school, she'd worked hard to understand everything numbers-related, and yet here she was, a high school graduate, still clueless about how to compute problems that began: *Two trains are leaving for Chicago at the same time. . . .*

This was the first time she was regretting her ignorance, because she really wanted to know exactly when she'd see Matt again.

Ivy figured it all out and chauffeured her to the airport to meet Matt's flight. Jacey watched his plane land and saw him race through the long corridors toward her. Jet-lagged and heartsick, neither of them was completely sure what time it was on their body clocks or even which coast they were supposed to be on. Neither cared.

It was enough that they were back together, locked in each other's arms, vowing never to let go.

It was more than enough that they actually did spend New Year's Eve together.

It was nothing short of a miracle that Jacey didn't end up checking her virginity at the gate.

The first time? It really was *all that*; it was everything Jacey had ever dreamed it would be. They didn't need candles, romantic music, or rose petals leading them to the bedroom.

This was about passion, not planning. It was about being with Mr. Right, not Mr. Right Now, no matter how the song went.

It made all the difference in the world—subconsciously, Jacey had always known this—to be with someone she trusted with all her heart, someone she was truly in love with, someone who couldn't get her off his mind, who couldn't live without her, no matter how huge their differences were.

Jacey and Matt spent the night and the entire next day alone together. They spent more time talking than doing anything else. There was a lot to say. Perhaps their painful week apart had been a wake-up call: if they couldn't really communicate, their relationship was doomed.

On the first day of the new year, Jacey Chandliss and Matt Canseco connected on a whole new level.

Matt blamed himself for everything. He apologized profusely for the way he had acted even after realizing how much loving planning Jacey had put into their earlier evening together. He was especially sorry for some of the things he had said.

Jacey forgave him, but she couldn't bring herself to say that she understood how he had believed the blog in the first place, even if she'd nearly made the same mistake.

Then Matt opened up even more. His anger had never really been about Garrett. It hadn't even been anger; it had been fear. The pictures in the blog had tripped a major insecurity switch. It didn't fit his image. Nor did it square with the way Matt saw himself.

Matt Canseco prided himself on being invulnerable. His instinct had been to stay away from anyone with the capacity to make him open up. He'd been very good at it, too. "Until you came along, Dimples."

He'd tried not to let her get under his skin, but Jacey had refused to take no for an answer. "You didn't give up on me. When I finally caved, I was on the lookout for you to betray me."

"And then the blog showed pictures of me with someone else," she filled in.

"Not just anyone else," Matt pointed out. "Someone you're obviously attracted to and feel a connection with. Maybe you even see a little of yourself in Garrett: the person you were before you won. But I should have listened to you, believed that nothing ever happened. Instead I jumped to all the wrong conclusions."

Guilt sliced through Jacey.

"Still, that's no excuse for what I did," Matt continued. "Crushing your Christmas Eve dream like that was harsh—"

"—I think you more than made up for it on New Year's Eve," she interjected with a smile.

"I hope so," he said softly.

There was more to say, on both sides. Matt admitted to being strangely weirded out by the candles, the flower petals, the negligee.

"I did something wrong?" she asked.

"Not you. I guess I felt—manipulated. Like you set the stage, and I was there to say my lines, do my part or something."

"You didn't like me being the director," Jacey speculated. "Is that it?"

"Afraid so, Dimples. My chauvinistic streak came out. I wanted to be in charge. I always have been and assumed I still would be. I'm twenty-one; you're not even eighteen."

"I'm a pushy little broad, aren't I?" She laughed and started a pillow fight. She had managed to lighten the moment. So, when she got around to preparing Matt for the photos of her and Garrett that would soon hit the Internet, he stopped her and said, "It's okay. I know they're fake."

## Jacey Kicked Off *Generation Next*!

It was bound to happen. Eventually, Jacey's loosey-goosey attitude was gonna catch up with her: the obvious bias toward "He's So Hot" Garrett; faking her comments to Todd about *Rain Man*, to cover up for the fact that she wasn't paying attention; leaving the show before the results were announced; and now, the pièce de résistance, hooking up with Garrett over the holidays! Is Jacey so self-absorbed she believes her actions have no consequences? Get real, starlet. You cost Todd his chance at winning. You crushed his dream. That's on you.

Finally, the producers have decided to do the right thing, and fire her. Jacey will not be on the judges' panel for the last show. But is that too little too late? And here's the big question: will her fling with Garrett also cost him the top prize?

# Chapter Seventeen

## A New Life

Busted by the blog. This time, the blogger nailed it, and made the scoop public before Jacey even knew she was fired.

Cinnamon called an hour after the posting. "Officially, you're off the show, because you skipped out before the results were announced," she explained. "It's already affecting your image. The buzz is that you're turning into another Lindsay: flighty and irresponsible. Are you sure Peyton can't tell them the real reason you left?"

Because Ivy had a meltdown, and Jacey chose to be there for her friend? No, that tidbit was not going public.

It was a moot point, anyway. The real reason Jacey had been fired from her volunteer job was her flagrantly unprofessional behavior with Garrett. It had gone way beyond the innocent lunch at the Farmers Market. This was about her clubbing in New York until all hours of the night; about retiring to her hotel with him.

But had her inattentiveness cost Todd his chance at winning?

"Should I call him and apologize?" Jacey worriedly asked her friends.

"No!" they all responded vociferously.

"You'd be admitting you screwed up," declared Desi. "Not smart."

"Besides, you were right. It *was* a bad choice to try and imitate a classic performance," Dash added.

"You'd be taking a bullet for something that would've happened anyway. Todd was a goner. End of story," Ivy said with finality.

Dodging a bullet was a more apt description of what had happened with Matt. Despite having seen the photos of Jacey and Garrett in New York and hearing the eye-witness accounts, Matt didn't believe any of it.

And there *was* an upside to being fired. Not appearing on the last show meant that no one could accuse her of affecting the voting one way or another. The less said and reported about Garrett and her, the better.

What freaked her out was hearing who would be

replacing her on the judges' panel. She ought to have guessed: the girl who'd come in second last year. Runner-up Carlin McClusky!

"It's like when Miss America is unwilling or unable to fulfill her duties, and the first runner-up takes over," Desi recited.

Jacey was not amused.

"Get over it, Jacey," Ivy advised. "We all know she's a publicity-hound. . . ."

"You forgot 'backstabbing bitch,'" Jacey grumbled.

"It's a one-hour TV show. The spotlight's on the performers. And that's the end of it," said Ivy.

"I've handed her a chance to be on national TV," Jacey groused.

What no one said: *maybe you should have considered that before you went gallivanting around New York with one of the finalists.*

Jacey was not in the best mood when the phone rang just then. She was completely unprepared to hear her stepdad's voice on the other end.

"Larry! Is everything okay?" she asked nervously.

"Everything's hunky-dory," he replied. "Mom's in labor."

"But . . . but . . . but . . ." Jacey sputtered, "the baby's not due for another two weeks!"

"Apparently, no one told him that. How soon do you think you can get here?"

Lawrence Jefferson Taylor was the most beautiful baby ever born. From his teensy-tiny tootsies to the doofy little cowlick in the middle of his otherwise hairless head, this child was perfection. Jacey Chandliss fell in love with her brother at first sight. Everything else in her life—career, *Generation Next*, the blog, Malibu, even Matt and her friends—seemed trivial and far away.

This new little life, forever connected to hers, was, at that moment, everything. The ferocity of her feelings took her by surprise. All during her mom's pregnancy, Jacey had been buying stuff for the baby: chic and pricey clothes, the trendiest carryall, the It stroller. She'd once even considered getting him his own domain name.

Now, all that seemed superfluous. All she wanted to do was protect him, cradle him, rock him and shower him with kisses. And she would have, 24-7, if not for the nurses at the hospital, and then the competition at home!

Her mom was exhilarated and exhausted. She and her husband had waited a long time for this miracle. It was unlikely she'd have another.

The infant was his father's first—and only—biological child. Jacey's rather large and imposing stepdad was overcome with emotion. When he wasn't holding the baby, he was wiping away tears or taking pictures. Larry Taylor, former college football player and current tool-and-die maker for the Ford Motor Company, bounced between weepy and gaga! The pleasure he took in his son was pure joy to see.

Maybe this was the difference between being a step-father and being a bio-dad. Larry took to fatherhood from the start, diving right into all of it, from changing diapers to bathing and burping the baby. He totally would have breast-fed if he could have.

Jacey took her turn with the newborn at every opportunity. She swaddled him, rocked him, even volunteered for middle-of-the-night diaper duty. She had, she bragged to her friends during their daily phone calls, the magic touch: she was best at soothing him when he cried.

"What's your secret?" Ivy asked.

"I don't coo at him. I talk to him, like a person," Jacey replied.

"Are you multitasking, rehearsing your lines from *Supergirl* with him?" Dash joked.

"Maybe she sings Pussycat Dolls songs to him," Desi giggled.

Jacey ignored the digs. "I just tell him how lucky he is, how wanted he is, and how loved."

In quiet moments with L.J.—that was what she'd decided to call him—Jacey talked to her tiny brother about all sorts of things. "The kind of stuff only a big sister would know," she said.

When he was only a week old, she advised him, "Stay away from mom's pea soup. She thinks it's her specialty. It's icky. Go for Larry's—that is, your dad's—barbecued chicken. It's outrageous. Also, *she's* the stickler for homework and putting your toys away. He's a total soft touch for buying ice cream, and new toys, and for letting you stay up past your bedtime."

"Do you think he really needs to know all that now?" Jacey's stepdad asked. He had just walked into the nursery, his arms piled high with brightly wrapped baby gifts.

"Never too soon to learn family secrets," Jacey said with a shrug.

"It sounds like you're trying to get everything in now, before you leave for home."

For a split second, Jacey didn't know what he meant. She *was* home. Or, because she'd been in California for the past year, did he think she no longer lived here?

Larry stacked the packages in a corner of the room. "You've got a lot of friends in Hollywood, Miss Chandliss. Your agent, publicist, that studio you're working with— they all sent gifts, one more lavish than the next. Silver picture frames from Tiffany, designer onesies, mono-grammed crib sheets."

"You make it sound like that's a bad thing," she said, a bit defensively.

"Not bad," he countered. "Just a little ridiculous. I mean, one of them registered Lawrence for his own domain name. Like he's gonna have his own Web site before he's a month old!" He shook his head. "It's like a competition, for who can spend the most money."

"Bragging rights are what Hollywood's all about." Jacey joked.

Her stepdad took her statement literally. "Hollywood, right. For better or worse, your world now, I guess."

*He makes it sound like I'm not part of this family anymore. What up with that?*

Of course, he hadn't meant it that way. Larry Taylor had married her mom nearly ten years before. He'd been nothing but wonderful to Jacey. He had provided for the family, driven her to skating, and gymnastics, and voice and acting lessons. He had never missed her school plays.

Perhaps they hadn't spent much father-daughter quality time together, nor had she confided her secrets to him, but he'd come into their lives and made everything better. And that was enough. He was, her mom always said, a big improvement over Jacey's bio-dad.

"There you are—my two men and my girl." Cece Chandliss Taylor strode into the nursery. "You're never going to believe who just called."

"The president?" Larry joked.

"Jacey's publicist, Peyton. That's her name, right? Three magazines have called her, offering to pay for photos of Jacey and the baby! Can you imagine?" She shook her head.

"Hollywood," Larry snorted. "It's bad enough they've plastered Jacey's face everywhere, trashed her at every opportunity. No one's getting near my son."

His fierce protectiveness made Jacey a little jealous. "It's just show business," she said evenly. "It's what they do. You can always say no, thanks; no need to get upset about it."

"Right—until the paparazzi start camping out on our lawn, looking to sneak a photo," Larry retorted.

"Overreacting much?" Jacey said. "It's not like Suri Cruise, or a Brangelina baby. It's not that big a story, or photo."

"They offered us five hundred thousand dollars, Jacey," her mom said. "As long as the photos are exclusive."

"I hope you told them where they can stick their money," Larry snorted.

"Of course I did, honey." Her mom waved dismissively.

Jacey was reminded of something Matt had said: most showbiz parents are totally in it for the money. If this didn't prove hers weren't, nothing would! Despite downplaying it to her folks, Jacey *had* been hyperaware of the sneaky press. They treated anything that involved her as a big scoop. To play it safe, she hadn't shared even a single personal photo with anyone, not even Desi, Dash, cousin Ivy, or Matt.

"I feel so blessed," said Cece. "Our family is complete." She slipped one arm around Jacey, who was cradling L.J., and the other around her husband.

Larry took the baby from Jacey and gazed into his son's angelic face. "Who do you think he looks like, Jace? I say he's got my nose and your mom's complexion. Hard to tell what color his eyes will be, but I'm betting little Baldie will have dark hair."

Jacey scrutinized the infant's tiny features. He definitely had his mom's almond-shaped eyes, and the one curl on his head was dark brown. "He totally has your nose, Larry," she confirmed. "And, maybe, my lips?" She turned to her mom for confirmation. "What'd I look like at his age?"

"You were all eyes and dimples, and those lips! You always looked like you were puckering—like this."

Cece mimicked fish-lips and laughed. "If you don't believe it, go get one of the old scrapbooks from the basement."

Jacey followed through with the suggestion. She ferreted out a scrapbook and flipped through it. Hmmm. Her mom was right. She would not have won any beauty contests at birth! All her class pictures were there: every Brownie troop photo, one from each and every recital, and naturally, a shot from every play she'd ever done. There were only a few pictures of Jacey and her parents.

Her mom looked so young! And *so* late eighties, with big hair, shoulder pads, and leggings. What a hoot! Her bio-dad was a pale-eyed redhead and could've totally passed for a metal rocker.

She was climbing the basement stairs with the scrapbook when a snapshot came loose. She caught it before it fluttered to the floor.

She froze.

The photo, a frayed three-by-three, pictured a boy and a girl, maybe around ten years old.

The girl was *her* . . . ? It was like looking into a mirror. She was all copper hair, big blue eyes, and dimples. She had Jacey's curvy lips and her smile! The boy was obviously her real father.

The picture raised goose bumps on Jacey's arms.

Jacey flipped the photo over. Someone had written, *Jacob and Jacqueline, on the site of our new playground, September 15, 1975.*

The kids in the picture were standing outdoors, in a weedy lot in front of a faded green clapboard house. It looked familiar. A crescent-shaped sign was posted above the front door. Jacey squinted to read it, but all she could make out were two capital *H*'s.

Was this her dad's boyhood home? Maybe she'd visited once. Clearly, the girl was her dad's sister, Jacqueline Chandliss. Jacey did not remember ever hearing about her.

She was all set to ask her mom, then thought better of it. With all the excitement surrounding the new baby, and with Larry around, it wasn't the best time. She stuck the picture in her back pocket.

When Cece flipped through the scrapbook, she declared, "See, I was right! Look at you! My dimpled doll-face. Didn't look a thing like me; she favored her father's family." She cupped her daughter's chin lovingly. "But in every other way, she's my girl, and her own person. And I—we—couldn't be prouder."

Cinnamon called that night. The casting for *Supergirl* was slated to begin later in the week. They needed Jacey to screen-test with potential cast members.

Matt had been calling and texting regularly, also wanting to know when she'd be back. He missed her.

Jacey had been with her family for nearly two weeks. It was time to head back west.

On her final night at home, Jacey couldn't help hogging little L.J. His slate-blue eyes were darkening! They were turning into a warm, beautiful brown.

"I have to leave tomorrow," she whispered to the infant as she rocked him. "But I'll come back soon. I'm your big sister, L.J. No matter what, never forget that you can always count on me, for anything. I promise to be there for you."

Her tears fell freely. Jacey placed the already sleeping baby in his crib and dimmed the light. She wandered into the kitchen, where Larry caught her a few minutes later.

"Hey, Jace," he said warmly. "Is something wrong? You look like you've been crying."

"Nothing. I'm just a little bummed to be leaving tomorrow."

"You'll be back soon, though, I hope," Larry said. "Hey, how 'bout I fix you one of my extracrunchy hot-fudge sundaes?"

Jacey smiled. She remembered the time when a bowl of ice cream could fix anything. Her stepdad obviously hadn't forgotten, either.

Jacey hadn't planned on being blunt, but after a few mouthfuls of the creamy concoction, the question popped out before she could censor herself. "When you married my mom, I was eight years old. Did you guys ever talk about you adopting me?"

Larry's spoon was suspended midway between the dish and his mouth. He put it down. "Wow, wasn't expecting that one."

Jacey laughed awkwardly. "I don't mean to put you on the spot. Maybe the baby made me think about it."

A wave of embarrassment washed over Larry's ruggedly handsome face, almost as if he'd been caught in a lie. He cleared his throat, wiped his face with a napkin, and toyed with his spoon. Finally, he said, "Sweetie? That's a question I'd rather you asked your mom. I'm sorry."

"It's okay," Jacey rushed to assure him. "No biggie. And for what it's worth, I wouldn't change a thing. You made my childhood perfect."

Larry kissed the top of Jacey's head before he went up to bed.

It was close to midnight when Jacey tiptoed into the baby's room again. She found her mom in the rocker, nursing L.J. Cece looked up and smiled as her daughter came in. "He's a good eater. Just like you were."

Jacey plopped herself down on the floor by her mom's feet and watched the tender scene. A sliver of moonlight played upon Cece's face.

"What's going on, sweetheart?" her mom asked after a few minutes.

"Nothing. It's not important—"

"You want to know why Larry never adopted you," Cece said gently.

*Okaaay*! So Larry had given her a heads-up.

"Of course, I'll tell you anything you want to know," Cece said. "I'm wondering why you're asking now. Is it just because of the baby, or is there something else?"

"I'm not sure," Jaccy said carefully. She didn't want to make either her mom or Larry feel as if she were being critical of them. Nor was she jealous of the way Larry acted toward the baby. Okay, maybe she had felt a little pushed aside when he'd said that stuff about Hollywood being her home, only that sounded petty and juvenile! She settled on, "Matt . . . you know: my, uh, boyfriend?"

Cece grinned. "He's really important to you, isn't he?"

Jacey blushed. Could her mom tell that Matt had been her first, and very recently? "I was telling him how great you guys are, and Matt wondered why I wasn't, you know, Jacey Taylor."

Cece didn't answer right away. She waited until she'd

finished nursing the baby and placed him gently back in his crib. She closed the door and sat down on the floor next to her daughter, hugging her knees.

Something about her mom's actions made Jacey uneasy. "What? Am I some black-market baby you stole from a third-world country before it was in vogue?" she joked lamely.

"First, don't *ever* think Larry didn't want to adopt you. He very much wanted that to happen. So did I."

"Only it didn't," Jacey said. All kinds of scenarios skittered through her head. Was there something in Larry's background, like a criminal record, that had prevented him from adopting her, or was it her fault? Had Jacey, as a confused eight-year-old, refused?

"Your father, Jacob, would never give permission." Cece stated it flatly.

It took a few minutes for that to sink in. "I—I— thought he disappeared after  he skipped out on us," Jacey stammered.

Cece pressed her lips together. "I knew where to find him."

"Oh." Jacey tried to wrap her brain around these new revelations. "Did he want to come back to us? Is that why he refused? Or was he being spiteful, because you'd met Larry?"

A bitter laugh escaped her mom's lips. "He did not want to come back. That I can assure you."

"Why'd he say no, then?"

"I never knew," Cece admitted. "Pride, maybe? Being obstinate? I could never understand it. We asked every year. He never changed his mind. As time went on, it seemed less important. The three of us did fine together, we were a good, solid family, and that was enough. More than enough."

Jacey was processing this information when her mom swung toward her and gripped her shoulders, forcing Jacey to look at her. "Tell me the truth. Has Jacob contacted you? Is that why you're asking now?" There was genuine fear in her mom's voice.

"No! Of course not," Jacey assured her. "I would have told you, right away!"

Cece sighed, relieved. "I never wanted to worry you, but it is something I've been concerned about. Especially after you won and went to Hollywood and got so famous."

"You thought he'd try to find me?" Jacey asked, surprised. "Why? So he could play the proud papa?"

"That," her mom admitted, "and since so much has been written about your finances—"

"You're afraid he wants money from me?" Jacey cut in.

"It's been known to happen," Cece said sagely. "Like with lottery winners."

Her mom was echoing what Matt had once said.

"Is that why you broke up, Mom?" It was a question Jacey had never asked before. "Over money?"

"No, nothing like that," Cece assured her. "We had problems from the start, and we just grew apart. In the end, he had other interests, things that were more important to him than you and I were. And then one day he left."

Jacey completely forgot to ask about the photo stashed in her jeans pocket.

## Jacey Runs from Tough Questions!

While controversy swirls around the Jacey/Garrett McKinley scandal, Jacey has gone into hiding. That's one way to avoid the tough questions: the coward's way. Everyone knows your mom gave birth, and you have a stepbrother, blah-blah-blah, very nice. Is that really an excuse to be out of town for half a month? Especially when inquiring minds want to know more.

# Chapter Eighteen

### And This Year's Winner of
### *Generation Next* Is . . .

"Good evening, ladies and gentlemen, and welcome to the show that makes tomorrow's stars. This! Is! *Generation Next!*"

When Jacey had been a contestant, she had found Sean Brean's opening routine merely cheesy. Now that she was a star, it made her cringe.

"We're coming to you *live*, from Hollywood, California," Sean exclaimed, "on the most exciting night of the competition, the one we've all been waiting for. In just two short hours, *you*, America, will choose a winner, the next big star! Will it be the pride of Tapdance, Texas? The lovely and talented Crystal Bleu? Or New York's equally talented and handsome Garrett McKinley? Talk about a tough choice! Luckily, you've got four experienced judges to help you make the call. Let's meet them!"

Jacey, of course, was not among them. She'd returned from Michigan four days earlier and was in her comfy Nick & Nora flannel pajamas in the living room of her Malibu beach house, surrounded by her best friends, stuffing her face with popcorn. Not for one second did she regret not being one of the judges. She was over the headaches, the headlines, and the scandal.

Against everyone's advice, she had sent former contestant Todd a note of apology. He'd written back, letting her off the hook for his ouster. The exposure he'd had on the show had already netted him two movie auditions. Todd Forest was on his way, hoping to become the next Will Ferrell. Jacey wished him luck and retired her guilty conscience.

All that needed to happen, two hours from now, was Garrett's winning, and Jacey could put the epic *Gen Next* drama behind her.

There was no way she wasn't gonna watch, though! She planned to raise a glass every time substitute judge Carlin made an ass of herself. Also, she was curious to see whether Garrett had taken her advice about doing the dramatic scene from *The Outsiders* and finishing up with broad comedy. Had Garrett even remembered? She hadn't been the only tipsy thespian that night.

The camera was now on Miss Sabrina, who really needed to lose her makeup artist. The older woman looked like a painted marionette, all red, concave cheeks and scarily scarlet lips.

"We've got a very special celebrity guest judge tonight," Sean announced breathlessly. "Meet last year's finalist, Carlin McClusky!"

Carlin's makeup, Jacey was bummed to see, was perfect. So was her spray-on tan. She shimmered in a white halter top, tossed her golden tresses, smiled brightly, and waved to the camera.

"Hi, everyone!" she chirped. "I am honored to be here for the most important night of judging. I owe my entire career to *Generation Next*. I just know both finalists are headed for amazing futures."

"What career?" sniped Jacey, hoisting a glass of iced tea.

"Not a word about Jacey?" Desi groused. She turned to Jacey. "That's just wrong. Someone should have given you props for all the shows you were part of!"

Dash didn't agree. "By mentioning Jacey, she reminds the audience about her and Garrett. That could only hurt him."

"Notice," Ivy said, "how they skirted around the fact that she lost to you!"

Jacey grinned knowingly. "She's totally in character. I expected nothing less. Or more."

"What is she *doing*?" Desi asked, flummoxed as Crystal pranced onstage. "What's up with the schoolgirl uniform and that pointer? That wig is weird, too. If she's gonna act out Britney's '(Hit Me Baby),' the skirt should be shorter, and the blouse should be tied."

"She's Hermione." Dash cut her off. "She's gonna do a scene from Harry Potter. And that's a wand, not a pointer."

"So where's—?" Ivy didn't get a chance to finish her sentence. Garrett, draped in a Hogwarts robe, wearing round black specs, was going to be Harry for this skit.

Jacey's stomach muscles clenched. Playing one of the best-known and most beloved characters of all time would be a major challenge for anyone! How could voters not compare him with Daniel Radcliffe? Garrett had to play younger than his real age, had to seem naive, thoughtful, and—gulp!—magical. Crystal, too, would be portraying a much-loved character, a character younger than herself. In most of the movies, Hermione had the best lines. So . . . was Ms. Bleu's strategy to showcase her strengths, or point out Garrett's weaknesses?

Jacey inched closer to the TV and upped the volume.

"It's from *Harry Potter and the Goblet of Fire*," Dash declared.

"How do you know?" asked Desi.

"Because it's the part about Hermione's campaign to free the house elves," he said.

The scene was a good choice, Jacey reluctantly conceded. Hermione displays her passion for equal rights, no matter who one is or what one looks like. If Crystal nailed the underlying emotion about Hermione's own issues— her Muggle, that is, nonmagical parents—she had done her job.

As the scene played out, Jacey was as tense as if she'd been onstage. Watching Garrett do an admirable Harry did not boost her confidence, because Crystal was flat-out phenomenal.

Not surprisingly, the judges agreed. Alex swooned, Lloyd applauded, even Miss Sabrina, who had never seen a Harry Potter movie, praised the passion Crystal had put into her speech.

Carlin raved, "That was so brave, Crystal, to play down your obvious beauty in the service of your girl-geek character. It shows you're willing to lose yourself in a part. You're so versatile! Go, you!"

"Go, *yeew*," Desi said, mimicking Carlin. "Please. Could she take up any more air time?"

"That's her agenda," Jacey said. "Keep the spotlight on herself, as long as possible."

When Garrett strode cockily onstage in a wrinkled black T-shirt and Levi's, his hair slicked back and a cigarette stuck behind his ear, Jacey knew instantly he'd taken her advice and would portray Dallas Winston in *The Outsiders*.

Only . . . Jacey sort of wished she could take back that advice. It occurred to her, too late now, that Cherry Valance—the wealthy girl who threw her soda at Dally in that scene—could seem like the more dramatic portrayal. And the audience might not rate Garrett's more subtle characterization as highly.

She mouthed the words to the scene along with him. Her friends rolled their eyes at her intensity.

Garrett rocked the scene; no one could take that away. He hadn't imitated Matt Dillon's classic performance; he'd modernized it and claimed it for his own.

Would the judges get that? Now Jacey wished she were there, or at least close enough to pass a note to Alex. Even without her insight, however, Alex (who probably had a crush on Garrett) still gave him high marks. Lloyd, thankfully, understood that it was harder to play the quiet, thoughtful character than the one who throws a hissy fit. As for Miss Sabrina, she praised Garrett's "delectable

James Dean." Only, she wasn't sure if he was doing *Rebel Without a Cause* or *Giant*.

Carlin McClusky's was the one negative voice. And Jacey wanted to reach through the screen and punch her. "Oh, Garrett," Carlin whined, putting on a show of pouty disappointment. "If you had to do *The Outsiders*, I so wish you'd cast yourself as Johnny! That scene where he perished in the fire . . ." Carlin actually placed her hands on her heart! "That would have been so memorable."

Jacey felt her insides churning. She wanted to call Garrett.

"And say what?" Dash asked.

"I'm sorry?" Jacey squeaked. "Or maybe, don't do the comedy bit I suggested for the finale?"

"You . . . *suggested*?" A look of horror washed over Ivy's face. "Please tell me no one knows you influenced him. In any way."

"We were—" Jacey stopped short of saying, "drunk." The less anyone knew about that, the better.

After the break, just long enough to give the home audience time to vote on the first half, the show returned.

For the final segment, Garrett was up first, which added to Jacey's uneasiness. When she'd confidently told him to "leave them laughing," she'd pictured his going after Crystal, giving the final performance of the season.

Well, at least he started them off laughing. Garrett gave goofily good belly laugh in the raucous 'n' rollicking *School of Rock*! He played against his to-die-for good looks as the flabby, head-banging loser trying to instill a rebel spirit in his students.

*Yessss!* Jacey clapped wildly, even whistled, when he was done. This was a side of himself he'd never shown before. "Chalk one up for versatility!" she shouted at the TV screen, pumping her fist. That performance had to earn Garrett serious kudos from the judges. Oh, if only she had been there! She would have compared him not to Jack Black, but to Tom Hanks, or Will Smith—movie-star icons equally at home with comedy, drama, adventure, action, Shakespeare, even! She would have announced that Garrett McKinley was the total package, the boy who could do it all. She would say that he should win.

Alex Treadwell was with her all the way. Jacey blessed the man for practically channeling her. "I laughed so hard I practically wet myself!" Alex said. "You killed!"

Lloyd was on board as well. "I'll hand it to you, Garrett. You showed me something there—a range we haven't seen from you before. You got your hands dirty for this character; you got silly. And it worked."

Miss Sabrina seemed to enjoy the performance, too, though the odds of her having seen *School of Rock* were on a par with those of her joining a rock band. "Brava! Brava!" was pretty much all Jacey could make out.

There was no way Carlin could criticize him this go-round.

Okay, Jacey thought to herself, Garrett's got it. He's got to win now.

Relief spilled from every pore. It was short-lived.

What Jacey hadn't counted on was Crystal, who did the one thing Garrett hadn't thought to do. Girlfriend strutted onstage in a sexy red bathing suit and did a scene from—the posse gave a collective gasp—*Baywatch*. She was all boobs and batting eyelashes. She was Pamela Anderson.

"No way!" Desi stamped her foot, outraged. "She can't do that."

"It appears that she can," said a stupefied Dash.

Ivy put her head in her hands. "Every guy in America is going to vote for her. Even the gay ones."

"Every girl will vote against her," declared Desi. "What's she proving is that her talent is in her—" She didn't have to finish the sentence.

Jacey felt sick—and responsible. She should have thought of this. It was so obvious! How hot had Garrett been in that tank top as *Grease*'s Danny Zuko? Sex appeal. Both finalists had it. Crystal had been cagey enough to use it. Someone should have advised Garrett to leave 'em panting, not laughing.

"He's doomed," Jacey groaned.

"Take it easy, Jacey," Dash said. "It could work against her."

It won't, thought Jacey. Crystal just put it out there. She might as well have worn a sign: *Vote for me, guys, you'll be seeing lots more of this!*

Some of the judges had to call her on it. Alex agreed that while a hot bod was an asset in this biz, he'd have been more impressed if she'd proved her allure by doing a scene from almost any Elizabeth Taylor movie.

Lloyd gave Crystal low marks for choosing a scene in which acting wasn't required. And Miss Sabrina sniffed, "This isn't the Miss America Pageant, dear."

It was Carlin who beamed like a proud coach. She applauded Crystal's daring and showbiz savvy. "You did the right thing, girl. With your looks, with that body, you showed moviegoers one big reason they should come see you. Being sexy never hurt Halle Berry or Beyoncé. Your future is so bright we'll all have to wear shades."

"Excuse me, I need to hurl," said Desi.

"That was a total stunt. It's got to work against her." Ivy sounded less than confident.

After a commercial, the host announced that

audiences had one hour to vote. During that time, *Generation Next* would air clips showing all of Garrett's and Crystal's weekly performances. "They knocked 'em out of the park tonight," he said, flashing teeth so white you could read by them. "But before you crown the big winner, remember to consider not just tonight's knock-'em-dead performances, but Garrett's and Crystal's entire bodies of work."

Had he deliberately emphasized the word *bodies*, or was Jacey being paranoid?

"We'll be back in one hour," he reminded viewers, "with your choice for America's Top Young Actor!"

Waiting was excruciating. While the others called and typed in their votes, Jacey paced and watched the clock. When she'd been in competition, Jacey had been a nervous wreck, sure, but she had also felt a strange sense of calm. She had known she'd done her best. Fate would decide whether or not she'd win.

Had she helped shape Garrett's fate? Would their rumored romance prove to be his undoing? Or would it all come down to Crystal's eye-popping boobs?

Finally, the longest hour in history was up. The show was back, live. Predictably, Sean stalled before announcing the winner, milking every ounce of drama and anticipation possible.

"And the winner . . ." He paused. ". . . Of *Generation Next* . . ." Another lo-o-o-ong pause. ". . . Will be revealed right after these messages!" Jacey wanted to reach into the big screen and choke the result out of him.

"Cool it, Jace," Dash said. "You know this is how it works. He's using the same script he used last year."

"That doesn't make it any easier!" Jacey shouted at poor Dash. "I'm sorry. I'm just really wound up."

"We couldn't tell," Ivy deadpanned. "But I'm not surprised you're making this all about you."

"I am not!" Jacey said indignantly, getting closer to Ivy's face.

Dash stepped between them. "Everyone thinks they can influence the outcome of a competition or game. It's just silly superstitions—ballplayers turn their hats backward; you think if you change the channel, it'll affect the outcome of a game. We're all guilty of that."

"No, Ivy's right," Jacey suddenly said. Her cousin had busted her. She was giving herself too much credit, elevating her own role in what was ultimately a national talent competition that she wasn't part of.

Garrett had gotten to the finals because of his talent, his looks, and his charisma. It had nothing to do with her. He would win this. He deserved to. The next words out of Sean's mouth were absolutely going to be—

"Crystal Bleu!"

Jacey had turned her back on the TV. She whirled around. "What? What'd he say?" For a moment, she calmed down. "That's the runner-up, right? She's the runner—"

Dash was grim.

Ivy stared at the screen, flabbergasted. "I wasn't serious when I said all the guys would vote for her!"

Desi pulled at her curls, "No fair!"

On TV, Garrett was hugging Crystal. Everyone was hugging Crystal.

## Was She Paid Off by Club Crystal?

I'm wondering, because Jacey could not have sabotaged Garrett McKinley any more if she'd actually been trying. What was she thinking? Between that first (at the time, funny) shout-out to Garrett's sexiness and those coast-to-coast hook-ups with him, did she not think voters would disapprove?

Here's who's at fault: *Generation Next* for taking too long to revoke Jacey's judgeship. If she'd been booted after that first open mouth–insert foot gaffe, Todd, Crystal, and Garrett might've had a level playing field. And Jacey, for playing the femme fatale to Garrett's naive newcomer. It was a foolhardy faux pas, proving fatal to his chances.

# Chapter Nineteen

## A Day of Rock and Revelations

Jacey was shocked. Shocked! She was still reeling from Garrett's *Generation Next* loss, and even more from his reaction.

Garrett seemed thrilled by the outcome, pumped beyond his wildest dreams, revved, and ready to begin the most exciting chapter of his life.

For that, he had Jacey to thank.

Jacey had called Garrett as soon as she could, expecting to console him, apologize for giving him the wrong advice, and take the blame for messing up his chances at winning. She had been ready to do all the talking.

Instead, Jacey did all the listening.

Garrett was more upbeat than she'd ever heard him.

He explained, "Spending so much time with you really opened my eyes. I saw exactly what my life would have been like if I'd won. I'd have been in the spotlight 24-7, always under scrutiny. Sheesh, any time I went on a date, it'd be front page-news. And all those tabloids and blogs, just itching to tear me apart. I don't know how you take it, Jacey, because I don't think I could. You're an amazing person to put up with it."

"But you lost—to Crystal!" Jacey was stunned. "You're not even disappointed?"

"Don't get me wrong," Garrett said. "I wanted to win the thing. I acted my butt off! But when it came down to it, and they said Crystal's name, all I felt was pure relief."

"So you're going home? Giving up acting?" she asked.

"No, of course not!" Garrett exclaimed. "Wait, no one told you?"

"Told me?" she echoed.

"Cinnamon Jones, your agent? I signed with her yesterday. She's lining up auditions for me. I might try out for a role in *Supergirl*! How amazing would that be?"

"Cinnamon's your agent now?" *When had that happened?*

"I'm staying in Hollywood, Jacey," Garrett crowed. "I'm going to try and make it here, to live my dream, like you're doing. Only, with no strings attached. Since I didn't win, I don't have to deal with an image. I can just be myself. And I owe it all to you."

After they said their good-byes, Jacey flipped the phone closed, unable to define her feelings. Garrett had gotten what he really wanted after all. As his friend, she should have been psyched. So why was she feeling taken advantage of?

The next day, an invitation arrived for Jacey via the strangest route: snail mail. In showbiz, that was like using the pony express. For that reason alone, Jacey assumed it was a solicitation, or a mistake. The fact that it was written in crayon intrigued her enough to open it.

### Dear Jacey Chandliss and Desi and Your Friends,

You are invited to be our special guests at a Talent Show we are putting on just for you. We want to say thank you for all the Christmas presents! Since you are an actress, we hope you'll like our talents.

Please come Thursday afternoon, at 2 p.m. Snacks will be served!

Love,
The Shelter Rock kids

How sweet! Jacey thought. She reread the invitation, feeling warm and fuzzy all over, and determined to get the truth out of Desi about Shelter Rock. Whatever Desi's motivation, the deal was done: Jacey had gotten attached to the place and to the kids. Since Dash couldn't find anything shady about it, she'd tell Cinnamon and her lawyers to do a thorough investigation. If they agreed that Shelter Rock was a truly worthy cause, Jacey would become its major benefactor. She would instruct Avalon Studios to give a big chunk of her salary to the charity. If she got more famous, she'd throw benefits for the place and invite all her celebrity pals. By that time, her family might be able to come out and participate, too. Which would be very cool indeed.

None of that was gonna happen, however, until a certain Desiree Constance Paczi spilled all.

"Now would be a good time," Jacey said as soon as she'd found Desi. The moonfaced curly-girl was at the kitchen table, doing her homework and snacking. She had just started a semester of taking courses at Santa Monica High School and hoped to earn her diploma as soon as possible.

Conveniently, Dash was there, too, helping her.

Neither would willingly give it up about Shelter Rock.

And neither seemed surprised by the invitation

to the talent show, though both were eager to go.

They'd have to be separated, Jacey determined. Dash could stonewall, but Desi would fold. She always did.

But she remained obstinate when Jacey cornered her later. "You contacted them back in November," Jacey reminded her. "You took me out there."

Desi crossed her arms defensively. "So? What's the difference how you got there? You know it's deserving. You want to be charitable. Why not there?"

"You're missing the point." Jacey dialed it down, since her righteous demands weren't working. "I'm not arguing that Shelter Rock isn't deserving, and I'm not contradicting you. I do want to help them. And I will. I just need to know how all this began. Why did I get asked to help and not other celebrities? And since my involvement began with you, I need *you* to tell me."

"I can't."

"Can't, or won't?" Jacey asked, as gently as she could.

There was no response at all this time. Desi pressed her lips together, as if to seal them. Which meant she was keeping someone else's secret. But whose?

Jacey tried empathy. "Des, did someone in your family, someone you know, live there? Is that why it's so important to you?"

Desi looked at Jacey as if she were nuts. "No way."

"Look, Des, I know your folks had problems. . . ." she began, not sure exactly where she was going with this.

"My family isn't, like—" Desi started to answer, but then clammed up. "We take care of our own," she finally said. "No one ever got dumped at a place like Shelter Rock, no matter how poor or sick anyone was. You know that, Jacey Chandliss."

"I do!" Jacey agreed. "Which is why it's so strange that you've been pushing me about this for months."

"Why can't you just forget that part of it?" Desi demanded.

"You know I can't, Des," Jacey said softly. "I need to know the truth."

"I promised, Jacey!" Desi sounded like a petulant second grader. "Everything's going so great. They love you! You love them! Please don't mess it up."

"Promised who? Did you know Rosalie Cross from before?"

"No." Desi hesitated a second too long—as if she were deciding whether or not to lie.

"Okay, not Rosalie Cross," Jacey said with a sigh. "Then who, who did you promise? What did you promise?"

"Not to say anything." Desi's bottom lip was quivering. Uh-oh. She was either going to cry or cave. Except that then Dash walked in and prevented any more leakage. "Don't badger her, Jacey, please."

"Fine. I'll badger you, then. You know a lot more than you're saying, Dashiell."

"You're right, Jacey. Desi and I both do. But there's nothing shady here; that I can promise you. It's all on the up-and-up. I would never have let you get near Shelter Rock if I wasn't a thousand percent sure you would be doing a good thing—a worthy thing. You could be helping a ton of kids. I know that's what you want."

"Good speech, but not good enough." Jacey was being obstinate.

Dash dug in. "If that's not good enough for you—" he began.

"You know what I mean! I'm thrilled to have found a good cause. I'm epically *unthrilled* at the two of you right now," Jacey said, frustrated.

Perhaps that was why Dash gently took her by the shoulders and gave her this crumb: "Let's go to Shelter Rock's talent show. If you still feel strongly, if you still insist on forcing Desi to betray someone's trust . . ." He purposely trailed off.

"Don't put it like that!"

"Dash, she's gonna find out soon enough, let's not attack her," Desi broke in.

She'd find out soon enough? As in, Thursday? "Are you saying that I'll find out whatever deep dark secret you guys are keeping, then?"

The First Annual Shelter Rock Talent Show rocked! It had been a long time since Jacey had gone to a talent show that she wasn't a part of. She'd forgotten how much fun it was. The kids were so cute! A little stage area with wooden benches and chairs for the audience sat next to the playground. The seats were filled with staff members, teachers, social workers, and family members.

Rosalie Cross ushered the posse over to the VIP section, a group of benches in the front row specially reserved for them. They were officially welcomed by all of the residents by way of an original song written by two Shelter Rock teens. Set to hip-hop rhymes, the beats were as good as anything done by the rappers dominating the music charts. If these kids got professional guidance and opportunity, who knew how far they'd go?

When Jacey mentioned her thoughts to Dash, he replied, "I know! But no one is looking to you for that kind of help. They really just want to thank you. This is pure, Jace. From the heart."

That became obvious as the kids took their turns at center stage. Using music that came from the CD players and iPods with docks that Jacey had given them for Christmas, the kids performed more hip-hop numbers and some rock and country tunes. Some displayed awesome break dancing skills. A group of girls did an intricate jump-rope routine to music that had Jacey's head spinning. There were stand-up comics in the group whose jokes, however silly, got more laughs than hit sitcoms!

"This talent show rules!" Jacey exclaimed to Rosalie, who'd sat down next to her.

"You can see how much joy your donations have already brought them," Rosalie remarked. "I haven't seen residents this upbeat and spirited in years. They had more fun planning and rehearsing, even, than they're having now. It gave them something to look forward to."

Jacey smiled. She gazed up at the sky, which was a late-afternoon azure. She inhaled. Even this acrid desert air carried the tiniest tinge of citrus. Before turning her attention back to the show, her eyes happened to fall on the front door of the main house. There was a crescent-shaped wooden sign above the door that said, *Welcome to Shelter Rock.*

Then it came to her: *That* was what it was! The sign— that was what had been so familiar from the picture that had fallen out of the old family scrapbook. Only, the sign in the photo hadn't said *Shelter Rock*. There had been two *H*'s in that one.

Then she remembered. Jacey leaned over to Rosalie and whispered, "Did you tell us that Shelter Rock used to be called something else?"

Rosalie's eyes were fixed on a pair of break-dancers. "Haven House," she replied. "Way before my time." The break-dancers finished their routine, and the small audience clapped enthusiastically.

Jacey's heart started to race. She had trouble concentrating on the last skit. She was thinking about the photo. Where had she stashed it? It'd been in her jeans pocket; then she'd stuck it in her bag. The same bag that was at her feet right now.

The *Galaxy Rangers* skit was the grand finale. Rosalie charged up to the stage and thanked the kids for the wonderful performance. The audience was on its feet. When the cheering died down, Rosalie asked Jacey whether she'd like to come up and say a few words.

Jacey thanked her lucky stars for her acting ability, because her mind was elsewhere. "I'm so touched," she said, placing her hands over her heart. "You've shown me what real love is all about."

She was thinking about the snapshot of a brother and sister, standing maybe just a few feet away from where she was right now. A brother and sister to whom she was obviously related.

A warning sign went up in Jacey's head: *Stop thinking. Danger ahead.* She paid no attention to it. The instinct for avoidance wasn't nearly as strong as the pull to dig the picture out of her bag. She waited until the kids had dispersed and just a few people remained outside.

Jacey took the picture out of her bag and looked from it to the playground and from the sign above the door to the one in the photo: *H.H.*

"Haven House. That's that it was called in the sixties. We used to call it Hell Hole." The voice came from behind her. It was male, and vaguely familiar; a voice she'd heard long ago. A part of Jacey wasn't shocked to hear it now. And when she spun around, she wasn't the least bit surprised to be staring into a pair of huge, ocean blue eyes, set deeply in the weathered face of a middle-aged man with copper-colored hair.

Jacey stood absolutely still.

Jacob Chandliss, or simply Jake, as the adoring kids and staff at Shelter Rock called him, pointed toward the house. "This is where we lived for most of our childhood. Me and my sister, Jacky. Your aunt." He paused, and it was as if time stood still.

"Jacky was very talented," Jacob Chandliss went on.

"She always dreamed of being an actress. Never got the chance. You look just like her, Jacey."

He reached for her. That was what broke the spell. Jacey fled. She would have run all the way back to Malibu if the Escalade, with Ivy at the wheel, hadn't caught up to her, if Dash and Desi hadn't hoisted her into the car and belted her in.

Her posse was talking to her, but Jacey refused to hear a single word. As soon as the car turned off the Pacific Coast Highway and on to her street, she unhooked the seat belt and ran. This time, they let her go.

She ran fast and hard, so all she could hear was the sound of her own panting and her sneakers pounding the pavement. She kicked them off when she hit the sand, and when she reached the water, Jacey dropped down on the wet sand and wrapped her arms around her knees.

# Chapter Twenty

## All Access Granted

Matt Canseco found Jacey sitting on the beach staring at the horizon. He came up behind her and draped his sweatshirt over her shoulders. Then he sat down and wrapped his arms around her.

He rested his chin on her shoulder, and Jacey pressed her back against his warm, bare chest. His body felt like a human cocoon, an outer shell to protect her against the elements, and she was grateful.

For a long time, they sat wordlessly watching the tide send ripples of saltwater toward their feet. Each time the cycle repeated itself, the tiny waves inched closer to them. Soon the water covered their feet, and eventually, it soaked their bottoms. They didn't move.

"I'm so sorry, Dimples," Matt finally said.

Jacey twisted around and looked up at him through a tangle of windswept hair.

"If I'd known," Matt said, holding her more tightly, "it never would have gone down like that."

"That's why they didn't tell you." Jacey found her voice. She had no more tears left to cry, no energy left with which to drum up righteous anger.

"Probably," Matt agreed.

"Do I have a target on my back that says, 'Use me'?" Jacey asked, staring back at the ocean.

"You got it the day you won on *Generation Next*," Matt said. "We all do, Jacey—all of us so-called celebrities. It's part of the prize package, the one no one tells you about."

"I got used to the spotlight, the paparazzi, the blog, even—to everyone knowing every move I make. But this feels different, like someone's getting hold of an all-access pass to my entire life, and using it, using me, for whatever they want."

"It must hurt like hell, baby," he murmured.

"I never understood why celebrities party all the time, drink every night, mess themselves up with drugs. I get that now. Maybe they feel as used as I do, and that's the only way not to feel anything," Jacey said.

"Been there," Matt confessed. "It never helps. You

always feel ten times suckier when you sober up. Eventually, you learn to protect yourself from the parasites, the people who only want what they can get out of you. And stick with the ones who'll stick by you."

"That's what my posse is supposed to be for," Jacey said. "But they ambushed me. They set me up and led me straight to Shelter Rock, where my own flesh and blood would try to use me."

"Oh, Dimples, I'm sure they never saw it that way."

"Desi and Dash—the two people I trusted most in the whole world. They let my father, who abandoned me, use me to get money. How could they do that?"

"They messed up, big-time," Matt agreed. "But I guess—I dunno, Dimples—they thought they were doing the right thing."

"On what planet is sucker-punching your best friend the right thing?" Jacey freed herself from Matt's embrace and twisted her body around to face him. "I don't get it."

"The thing is," Matt said, inching ever so slightly away from her, as if afraid the next words out of his mouth might set off a tinderbox, "I'm not defending them, but I can see why Desi would have fallen for your father's story, and why Dash went along with it."

"Enlighten me," Jacey said, feeling the burn of anger start in her belly.

"Your father was using you—absolutely—he used them, too, as puppets," Matt said. "He pulled their strings to get to you."

"Desi's easy," Jacey said. "She's a soft touch. You tell her a kitten's up a tree, and she'll climb it without looking up first. She just believes in the goodness of people. It's one of the reasons"—Jacey felt herself choking up—"that I love her so much and need her here with me. Desi would fall for any hoax—but Dash? He's the one I don't get. He's the smart one."

"See, here's the thing, Jacey. It wasn't a hoax. Not in the sense that you were tricked by your father because of any greed on his part."

"Please don't refer to that man as my father," Jacey said snippily, turning away from Matt again.

"Jacob Chandliss wasn't out for selfish gain," Matt continued. "He wanted money to help kids in need. He saw a way to get it. Unfortunately, that way was you."

"Yet he didn't just come and ask me for it, did he? He had to do an end run around me, and use my friends to get to me. That sucks."

Matt knelt in front of Jacey and pinned her with a hard stare. "Would you have helped his cause if he'd asked you directly?"

It was a rhetorical question, and they both knew

it. Jacey focused her gaze on a point beyond Matt's shoulder.

"Bottom line," Matt concluded, "is that the guy did a crap thing for a good cause."

"Bottom line," Jacey returned fire, with way more power than she'd have thought possible, "he bailed on us! He left me! Me and my mom. Just walked out, left us with nothing. She had to work two jobs. For three years I spent more time in Ivy's house than in my own. The guy abandoned one kid—that'd be me—to go help a bunch of others. It's worse than hypocritical: it's evil. And now I'm supposed to pitch in? I don't think so. He stunk up the good cause, as far as I'm concerned. Now it's backfired on him. I'm not supporting it."

"So you're going to pull your support for Shelter Rock?"

"I have to. If I don't, it's admitting I'm okay with his methods. He wins."

"But the kids lose."

Jacey glared at him.

"I'm sorry, Dimples, but that's the simple truth."

"There's nothing simple about it, Matt." She jumped up and started walking down the beach along the shoreline.

Matt followed and fell into step next to her.

Jacey hadn't realized she had a destination, but she

was almost past the dunes at the cove—their cove—when she stopped short and turned to Matt. "The only reason people have too much money is because they haven't given enough away. Rosie O'Donnell said that, and it . . . it struck a chord with me."

"I know. I get that better than most people," Matt said.

"When I won on *Generation Next* and got my first movie role, in *Four Sisters*, it was like, suddenly I had all this money. Mom and Larry put it right into a college fund for me. It meant they wouldn't have to take out any loans. It was a big deal at the time. We were all thrilled. No one ever imagined that could happen so easily!"

"You're talking to someone who never had much growing up," Matt reminded her. "Then, suddenly, you make a movie, and it's like winning the lottery. You have more than you ever dreamed of—"

"—And that's supposed to make you happy." She finished the sentence for him. "Because everyone wants a lot of money, right? As much as you can get, right? I thought I did, too. It was so weird to find out that I didn't—that it didn't mean that much to me, and it never would. Unless I could do some good with it."

"Enter the worthy-cause brigade," Matt said knowingly, and he put his arm around her once again.

A never-ending, unyielding stream of people had

solicited her support—read: money—for so many causes it was mind-boggling. Jacey wanted to do the right thing. That was the reason she'd asked Dash to help. She'd already donated thousands to help find cures for all manner of diseases, to help the environment, and to save animals.

But there was no cause she really felt connected to. Nothing she was doing that allowed her to see tangible results, like the joy in the faces of the kids earlier that day, and let her know that she'd helped bring some good into their lives. How freakin' ironic that the one cause she should feel good about had turned into this . . . trap?

Evening had fallen. Jacey hadn't even noticed the sun setting over the ocean. It was time to go back to the beach house, get out of her wet clothes, and get blitzed on something stronger than iced tea—and, maybe, cuddle with Matt for the rest of the night and not think about anything.

She looked toward Matt, who was rummaging around trying to find something stuffed in his pocket.

"Desi said to give you this," he said.

He offered her a white envelope. The writing on the front had gotten smeared from being in Matt's pocket when they were sitting in the water. Jacey made no move to take it.

"Do you want me to read it to you?" Matt asked.

"Whatever." She pretended not to care—or to sense who'd written it.

Dear Jacey,

Please don't be angry at your friends. If you have to be angry at anyone, it should be me. I deserve all the rage you have ever felt toward me, and more. But I would like to tell you a story. I wasn't sure you would listen to me, so I wrote it down.

As you no doubt have figured out, I am the director of Shelter Rock. My twin sister and I were left here by our parents when we were young— they dropped us off one day and didn't come back. Our lives here were less than happy. But I'm not looking for your pity. When I found out you were on that TV show, I started to watch it. I hadn't seen you in years, and it floored me just how much you looked like my sister. I voted for you, just so you know.

I won't take up your time with boring details about my life, but I would like you to know I have dedicated the rest of my life to making things better for children who are in the same position today that I was in many years ago.

When I read all the interviews you gave about wanting to donate to charitable causes, I thought I could take a chance and ask you to help out Shelter Rock. I knew you wouldn't talk to me. So I went behind your back and got your friend Desi to listen to me. Well, you know how it went from there. I can only hope you don't take your anger out on the children here who need you, and that you can find it in your heart to forgive your friends.

Jacob Chandliss's letter, perhaps because she was hearing it read by Matt, did not enrage her. It didn't make her want to grab it away from Matt, tear it into tiny pieces, and throw it out to sea.

She didn't do that, at any rate, until her friends showed up. Matt had just finished reading when Desi, Dash, and Ivy—a united front—came around the rocks. All at once the anger rose in her, and in seconds she'd shredded the letter and thrown into the waves.

"He wrote it yesterday," Desi said to Jacey's back. "Before the talent show. He had a feeling you wouldn't hang around to let him explain. So he gave it to me. I figured Matt was the only one with a shot at getting it to you. Maybe it'll help. If not today, then tomorrow."

Tomorrow. Another day would dawn, another brilliant, perfect Malibu day, with its golden promises. Tomorrow, Jacey would call her mom and tell her everything.

"Ironic, isn't it?" Jacey would say. "You were right. He did contact me. He did want money, after all."

Jacey turned around to where Matt, Desi, Dash, and Ivy were standing, waiting for her—waiting also to apologize, and to explain. Jacey let them, but she didn't listen. Jacey remained lost in her own thoughts—and anyway, she knew what they were going to say.

People often knew what they needed, but they didn't

always go about getting it the right way, without hurting someone. That didn't excuse Jacob Chandliss, even if he had used her to benefit needy kids, to right an ancient wrong that had been done to him; it would never erase the fact that he'd abandoned her. There weren't enough tomorrows for her to forgive him.

Tomorrow. She gazed over the dunes to where her beloved beach house sat. How empty it would be without her friends, and without her soul mate, Matt.

And Jacey Chandliss instantly understood.

Maybe it would take more than one tomorrow, but she'd forgive her friends. Desi, Dash, and Ivy occupied places in her heart so deep that to cut them out would have been slicing out a part of herself.

Tomorrow, she would send a check to Shelter Rock, and later on she would direct a portion of her *Supergirl* salary to that charity. At the end of the day, abandoning the Shelter Rock kids, spiting those kids who so clearly and instantaneously benefited from her generosity, was not something Jacey Chandliss could do.

Jacey slipped her arm around Matt's waist, then extended her other arm toward Desi, who immediately took it. Dash and Ivy moved in close. Jacey's family in Michigan was no less dear to her than her family here in Malibu.

Families messed up—sometimes, really badly. But in the end, you forgave one another, and that was what made you whole.

Jacey's gaze settled on dark and dreamy Matt Canseco. She'd been right to fight for that relationship. Matt truly had her best interests at heart, and had from the moment they'd met. For Matt, it was all-access granted, now and forever. For the first time in many hours, she felt a smile lighting up her face. Jacey Chandliss really was so pixie dust. She so had it all.